D1029087

The Baitchopper

SILVER DONALD CAMERON

The Baitchopper

Illustrated by Alan Daniel

James Lorimer & Company, Publishers
Toronto 1982

Juv. PS8555.A42414 B35
1982

Canadian Cataloguing in Publication Data

Cameron, Donald, 1937-
  The baitchopper

(The Adventure in Canada series)

ISBN 0-88862-599-5 (bound). - ISBN 0-88862-598-7 (pbk.)

1. Trade-unions - Fishermen - Nova Scotia - Juvenile fiction. I. Title. II. Series.

PS8555.A42B34   jC813'.54   C82-094981-7
PZ7.C35Ba

0-88862-599-5   cloth
0-88862-598-7   paper
Design: Michael Solomon

**Teacher's guide available from the publisher.
Write to the address below.**

The
Adventure in Canada
Series

James Lorimer & Company, Publishers
Egerton Ryerson Memorial Building
35 Britain Street
Toronto, M5A 1R7, Ontario

Printed and bound in Canada

This book is for all my favourite kids,
including Ronnie and Rene and Paul and
Patty and Peggy and Rodney and Paula
and Melanie and Kelly and Jerry and Paul
and Putt Putt and Robert and Kevin and
Krista and Michael and Belinda and
Samantha and Tanya and Melissa —
and particularly Everett Jr. and John, who
were there, Dohn Allan, who was born the
day the book was finished, and above all for
Maxwell and Ian and Leslie and Steven
and Mark Patrick Terri-yoyo Hamburger
Cameron

The author wishes to acknowledge his gratitude to the Canada Council, without whose generosity and encouragement this book could not have been completed.

1

"HEY!" said Denny. "The *Albatross* is in!"

Andrew looked down the government wharf where his cousin was pointing. The big steel fishing dragger, streaked with rust, was unloading fish at the fish-plant wharf.

"*Gannet* should be in pretty soon," said Andrew. "They went out about the same time."

"Hope so," Denny grinned.

Denny's father was mate on the *Gannet*, another big offshore trawler which went out fishing for two weeks at a time, far off the Nova Scotia coast. When Denny's father came home it was always an occasion. The offshore draggers fished all year round, in winter storms and ice. It was cold, hard, dangerous work. Lately the offshore men had been grumbling about the danger and the long hours of

1

work for very little money, and wondering what they could do about it.

"Listen!" said Denny.

Andrew heard it, too — the distant wail of a siren, a sound the boys hardly ever heard in quiet little Widow's Harbour.

"Comin' this way," said Andrew.

"And fast."

The siren grew louder, and then a white van with blue and red markings swept around the corner by the garage and down onto the fish-plant wharf.

"Ambulance!" said Andrew. "Let's go see what's happened!"

The two boys ran down behind the ambulance, which had pulled up right beside the ship. Two men walked down the gangway from the ship to the wharf, carrying a stretcher. The man on the stretcher was tossing from side to side and moaning. His left arm was outside the blanket, and they could see blood all over the bandage that covered his hand.

"That's Freddy Quinn!" said Denny. The boys ran up beside the ambulance. Louis Bond was handing the stretcher to one of the ambulance men. They slid it inside the ambulance, clapped the door shut, and turned on the siren again as the ambulance turned around and raced off the wharf. All the fishermen from the *Albatross* were gathered around, their faces grim.

"What happened?" Denny asked Louis.

"Got his hand caught in a winch," said Louis.

"Steel cable was wrappin' onto the winch and cut off three fingers."

"Three fingers!" Andrew could feel his stomach turning.

"And Freddy won't get nothin' for them fingers, neither," said another fisherman. "That's how much the company cares." He turned and spat towards the company's office building. "Bunch of vultures."

Andrew felt the heavy tug and trembling shudder of his fishing line in the water as another pollack struck his hook. With a sharp tug he set the hook firmly in the fish's mouth and reeled it in. Jerking and struggling in the air, the young pollack slapped against the side of the wharf as it came up. Andrew flipped it on the deck, stamped on its head with his rubber boot to kill it, plucked the hook out of its mouth and reached for another piece of bait as Denny took the quivering pollack.

"Another one, that's all we need," grunted Denny. "No point bein' greedy."

"Yeah," said Andrew, lowering his line back into the water. He could see the sleek, streamlined backs of the fish milling around in the water at the bottom of the pilings. Whenever the fish plant was working you could count on the pollack. They came to eat the fish wastes that came pouring out of the plant through a big steel pipe. His mother could make a wonderful meal out of pollack, which meant his father could sell the more expensive fish that he

4

caught with *Dolly C.* Every little bit helps, his father liked to say.

"Your folks want some of these, Scott?" Denny asked, cutting off the pollack's head with a hard stroke of his knife. Then he flipped the fish over to run the blade up its belly, opening it as though it had a zipper, and finally scooping the innards into a small pail.

"No," said Scott. Scott Guthrie was a small, wiry, blond boy who looked almost frail. Strong, though, for the size of him. Scott was squinting into the sunlight. Two boats were coming slowly out of the Tiddle, the narrow passage behind the fish plant where many inshore fishermen kept their boats. These two boats seemed to be tied side by side.

"Isn't that your Dad's boat, Andrew?" Scott asked.

Andrew looked over where Scott was pointing.

"Yeah, with Jimmy Parker's," he said. "Which one's towin'?"

"Looks like Jimmy's," said Denny.

"Must be something wrong with *Dolly C.*" Andrew's heart thumped inside him. It wasn't just that he knew how much the family depended on that boat, which was how his father made his living. It was *Dolly C* herself, which Andrew thought was certainly the most beautiful boat in the harbour, with her high, flaring bow and her low, shapely stern. As Jimmy carefully nosed the two boats in to the wharf, Andrew noticed that *Dolly C*'s motor was silent. Phonse Gurney stood in the open stern of *Dolly C* with two lengths of rope. Andrew dropped his rod and ran to catch one. Scott caught the other.

"What's the matter?" Andrew called to his father.

"Fouled the prop," Phonse answered. "Guess we'll have to put her ashore."

"What's that?" Scott asked.

"Got something caught in the propeller," Andrew explained. "Likely an old piece of rope or something. So the boat won't move—"

"I know *that*," said Scott indignantly. "But what's putting her ashore?"

"We'll run her up on the beach at high tide," he said, making *Dolly C*'s stern rope fast around the top of a piling. "Tie her alongside the wharf. Then when the tide goes down she's sitting there on the beach, and we can get at the propeller to work on it."

"That's not so bad, is it?"

"Lose a day's fishing," Andrew shrugged. Can't help it, though. You can't breathe underwater, so you got to put her ashore."

"Ha!" shouted Scott. He whirled on his heels and ran up the wharf as fast as he could go. Andrew watched him, open-mouthed. Scott ran off the wharf, across the road into the back yard of the Anglican rectory, and vanished.

A battered old van bounced through the pothole at the end of the wharf and clattered towards them. When it stopped, a man got out. He was square and stocky. He wore old blue jeans and a heavy work shirt. His hair was cut very short, and the word *MOTHER* was tattooed on his left forearm just above his wrist.

"Hi, Buck," said Andrew.

"How are you doin', Andy?" said Buck. He looked down into *Dolly C*. "You got troubles, Phonse?"

"Yes," said Phonse. "Got something wrapped around the wheel."

"Oboy," said Buck. He turned and backed down a ladder into the fishing boat. Andrew and Denny followed him.

Buck Poulos was the president of the Allied Fishermen's Union. With three other organizers he had driven all the way from British Columbia, right across Canada, to see whether Nova Scotia fishermen might want to join his union. It had taken them a week to complete the trip, sleeping in Buck's van. The other three men had gone off to talk to fishermen in other Nova Scotia ports. Buck said he would stay in Widow's Harbour until the union got established.

The men in the village had had a couple of meetings with Buck. Phonse had reported that they were setting up a local branch of the union, and that he was vice-president. Andrew and Denny didn't quite understand it. For one thing, Andrew always thought unions were big, and far away. But the fishermen talked as though this union was something like a fishermen's club. For another thing, the TV news always talked about unions being powerful. But one man in work clothes, driving around in an old van — that hardly seemed powerful. When he had asked Buck about this, Buck had laughed.

"Well, a union is just people working together," he had said. "And when a lot of people work together, they can really do things. You couldn't pull a car out of a ditch yourself, but forty fellows like you wouldn't have any trouble with it."

Now Buck was sitting on the engine box, talking with Phonse and Jimmy.

A shadow fell over the boat, and they all looked up. Scott was standing on the edge of the wharf with his father. Father Guthrie, the Anglican priest, was a tall, sandy-haired man with thin glasses. He was wearing an open-necked blue shirt and a pair of dress pants. He had only been in Widow's Harbour since Christmas, but he already seemed to belong.

"What's this I hear about your propeller being fouled?" Father Guthrie asked.

"Tee-totally jammed up," nodded Phonse. "I must have picked up an old bit of rope in the Tiddle there."

"Scott tells me you're planning to beach her."

"Pretty well all I *can* do," Phonse said.

"Well, now," said Father Guthrie. He looked at the sky for a moment, then looked back at Phonse. "A diver could go under there and clear away that rope in ten minutes."

"Sure," said Phonse, "but we got no divers in Widow's Harbour."

"Well," said Father Guthrie, almost shyly, "actually we do. I'm a diver myself."

"*You* are!" said Jimmy.

"I learned in the Navy, years ago. That's one reason I wanted to come here. I thought my wife and I might take it up again."

"So that's why you took off like that!" said Andrew. Scott just grinned.

"Never heard of a priest who was a diver," said Phonse. "You really think you can clear that prop?"

"I've done it before," said Father Guthrie. "You want me to try?"

"You bet I want you to try!"

Half an hour later Father Guthrie sat on the stern of *Dolly C.* He looked more like a spaceman than a priest, Andrew thought. He had tanks on his back, a hose in his mouth, and he was dressed in a black rubber suit with a hood that covered his head. He put one hand over the thick glass mask that covered his eyes and nose and rolled backwards into the water. There was a tremendous splash, and a boiling foam of bubbles. Andrew peered over the side of the boat. He could see the priest's legs slowly moving, with the long black fins on the feet. Then there were some more bubbles, and the priest's head popped up through the water.

"It's a piece of fishnet," called Father Guthrie. "No problem." He held a hose in his hand, put the end of it straight up in the air, and sank again. He was down a long time.

"Hi, Ernie," said Buck. Everyone looked up. Ernie Hendsbee, one of Andrew's school mates, was standing on the wharf, looking down into the boat.

"What's going on?" Ernie asked.

"Scott's father is clearing the prop," said Buck. "Come on aboard."

Father Guthrie's head bobbed up again.

"Got it," he said, hauling a length of net out of the water. "I think she'll work now. Give me a hand up, will you?"

Buck and Jimmy reached down and pulled. The priest scrambled up the side of the boat and rolled onto the deck. He slipped out of his heavy tanks and his belt with the lead weights on it. Then he pulled off his bulky mittens, his mask, and his flippers. Andrew looked at his suit. It was made of thin foam rubber, and it clung to him like an extra skin.

"I'm getting a wetsuit this summer," Scott said. "Eh, Dad?"

"That's right," nodded Father Guthrie.

"You're some lucky," said Ernie enviously, squatting down to look at the dials and gauges on the diving tank.

"I got a mask and flippers already," said Scott.

"How come you use a suit?" Andrew asked.

"In a wetsuit, the water trickles in next to your skin," Father Guthrie explained. "But it can't get out again, so it warms up, and the suit keeps it warm. It's the only way you can swim in cold water for any length of time." He wiped his hands on a rag and turned to Buck. "How's the union coming along?"

"You should ask Jimmy, here," said Buck. "He's the president of the local. We're going to talk to the company next week. But there's two draggers still out right now, and we want their crews signed up first."

"How do you think you'll make out?"

"I don't know," Buck said. "In any other business, they've *got* to bargain with you. That's the law. But in fishing, the law says you're not an employee, you're a partner with the owner of the boat. Well, that may be fair enough with little inshore boats like *Dolly C* here that just sell fish to the company. But it's sure not true with those million-dollar draggers that are actually owned by the fishing companies."

"Will the company bargain, though, if the law says they don't have to?"

"They did out West. But you've got to be strong enough to shut down the plant. If the fish companies can't get any fish, they can't make any money. So they'll bargain. That's why we want *all* the fishermen in the union first," Buck nodded at Phonse, "including the men who own the inshore boats."

"They say you're a Communist," said Father Guthrie.

Buck laughed. "They'll say anything to make me look bad. I used to be a Communist, but I'm not now. I'm still a socialist, though."

"What's a socialist?" asked Scott.

"If a business is big enough to control the life of a community, a socialist would say the community should own it," said Buck. He waved a hand at the fish plant. "Who owns that plant? Rich people in England and the United States and Ontario. All they care about is whether it makes money. They don't care what it does to the people down here. I believe the people here should own it." Buck looked the priest straight in the eye. "I don't believe in God, either, by the way."

Andrew looked quickly at Father Guthrie. What would he say?

The priest laughed. "When God created you, Buck, I don't think He put anything in the contract that said you had to believe in Him. He left you free to make your own errors."

Buck chuckled and shook his head.

"I believe you're all right," he said.

Andrew walked over to where Ernie was still examining Father Guthrie's diving gear.

"Pretty neat," Andrew said, pointing. "How hard is it to learn diving?"

"Not very hard," said Father Guthrie. "You can't get certified until you're sixteen, though."

"I'd like to learn it," said Andrew.

"Me, too," said Ernie.

"You can try my stuff, if you want," Scott offered.

"Promise?" said Ernie.

"Promise," said Scott.

2

"YOU lost!" cried George Jackson. "You lost, you lost, you lost!"

"We didn't lose!" shouted Andrew. He was so angry that his eyes were smarting. He could hardly even see George and the others. "It's only the start! Buck said it's only the start!"

"Who cares what a Communist says?" shouted George. "He's gonna get run out of town anyway!"

Andrew took a run at George, but George danced away, laughing. All the other kids were jeering at him, too. Then the bell rang, and Mr. Thurgood shouted at them. They lined up to go back into school. Andrew looked at the hair on the back of George's neck and wondered if he could get in a punch without Mr. Thurgood noticing.

Someone behind him pinched his arm, and twisted. Andrew cried out. Mr. Thurgood glared at him. Andrew turned to see who was behind him. Jeff Ritcey.

He couldn't think about math. He sat at his desk, staring at Mr. Thurgood and not seeing anything. The teacher's voice was like a distant buzzing in his ears. He kept thinking of what he should have said, what he should have done.

You lost!

We didn't lose, he told himself angrily. But it didn't sound very good, either. He thought about Skinner, the plant manager. He could almost see him standing behind his desk, wearing a white shirt with his tie loosened at his throat, talking to Buck, Jimmy Parker, Russ Ryan, and Phonse.

"I'm sorry, gentlemen," Skinner had said. "But the law says you don't have any right to a union. You're fishermen, you don't have unions."

Wait a minute, Buck had told him, almost all the fishermen on your boats are in our union —

"I know all about about you, Poulos!" Skinner had said, his voice rising. "You've got quite a reputation. You're the kind that wants to destroy everything this country stands for."

"I don't expect you to like me," Buck had replied. "But your men have formed a union, and they want to bargain —"

"Listen, Poulos," Skinner had interrupted. "This company has been good to this town. We provided these people with a good livelihood until you came along and started causing trouble. Now get out of here. You're trespassing on company property."

"Hey, hey, hey!" Jimmy had cried. "We're just talkin' now, no harm in that."

"I'm not talking to any of you," Skinner had said. "You've taken up enough of my time. Tie up the boats, if you think you can. If you're as strong as you say you are, then tie up the boats."

"We just might," Phonse had growled.

"Go ahead. Now get out of here."

Buck had looked at the other three. They had all shrugged, and turned for the door.

"Oh, one more thing, gentlemen."

The union men turned to the manager.

"Yes?" said Buck.

"Not you, *Mister* Poulos. Ryan? Parker? You're fired. And we won't be buying any more fish from you, Gurney. That's all. Get out."

So Russ and Jimmy had no jobs, and Phonse had no place to sell his fish. Buck sounded cheerful about it, but it didn't look good to Andrew. In Widow's Harbour the company always got pretty much what it wanted. George and Jeff thought the union had lost. If it turned out to be the end of the union, it would be the end of three families, too. They'd have to move. Jimmy, Russ, and Phonse would never find work in Widow's Harbour if the company didn't want them to.

Maybe his father had made a mistake.

Maybe they had lost.

"Andrew!" called Mr. Thurgood. "I asked you a question!"

"Sorry," said Andrew, not looking up.

"When I speak, I expect you to listen," said Mr. Thurgood. "In this classroom, Andrew, the boss is still the boss. There's no union here."

The class giggled.

"Should be," Andrew muttered.

"I heard that," snapped Mr. Thurgood. "You'll come back here at three o'clock, Andrew, and think about whether that was a smart thing to say."

"Yessir," said Andrew. Another detention! His mother would have something to say about that.

"Stop playing with your food, Andrew," said Laura Gurney. "What's the matter with you, anyway?"

"Nothing."

"How come you want us women at the meetin'?" Laura asked, turning to Buck.

"Because whatever we decide, the families are going to suffer the consequences," said Buck. "We want to hear what you think, right from the start. You're the one that's going to have to feed this family on strike pay, if it comes to that. A strike would affect you and Andy a whole lot. If you aren't behind it, we'd be better off knowing about it now."

"Well, are you going on strike or what?" Laura demanded.

"That's up to the fellows. Whatever they decide."

"So I guess we're all in this together, then," said Laura. "All right. Andrew and I'll be there."

The community hall was packed with fishermen and their families. The thin blue haze of cigarette smoke made Andrew's eyes smart. His father was up at the table in front with Buck and Jimmy. Andrew sat with Laura at the back. Denny was sitting beside him with his father Leo. Andrew saw Father Guthrie leaning against a side wall, talking to a couple of fishermen. Jimmy called the meeting to order and asked Buck to report what had happened in the meeting with Skinner. Then Jimmy said, "That's where she stands. Now, what are we gonna do about it?"

"Go on strike," called Louis Bond. A murmur of agreement ran through the hall.

Louis got up and said that he didn't think there was any other way to get Skinner to listen to them. And he didn't think there was any other way to get Jimmy, Phonse, and Russ back to work either. If the union just lay down and let Skinner walk over it, there wouldn't be any good in having a union at all.

"What are we gonna live on, if we go on strike?" demanded Ambrose Hendsbee. Ambrose was a red-faced man with an unshaven black stubble on his chin, and shiny black hair. Ernie was his nephew who lived with him. "You go on strike so's the company don't make no money. That's all well and good, but *you* ain't makin' no money either, so what are you gonna live on?"

Andrew craned his neck to try to see Ernie. There he was sitting beside his uncle, looking up and listening to what Ambrose said.

Buck turned to Ambrose. "Normally you'd have strike pay, because you'd have been putting some money aside in case you did have to strike. But nobody expected this strike — if we have a strike — so you'd have to earn money other ways as you go along. Ask other unions for help. Hold rallies and bingos. Get donations. One thing we've done out West is to sell fish in the cities, off the backs of pickup trucks. People like fresh fish, and it's hard to get in the city. That gets your story out, too. The newspapers and TV stations see what you're doing, and they'll come down and take pictures and write it up."

"We could do that," Phonse said. "Lots of us here got inshore boats. We could catch some pile of fish with all these fellers to work on 'em."

"But we don't *want* no strike!" cried Ambrose.

Then Uncle Alfred stood up, several rows of seats ahead of Andrew. Uncle Alfred was his father's oldest brother, a huge, weatherbeaten man with big knotted hands. Alfred fished with Phonse, and his son Jud fished on the *Gannet* with Leo. Alfred was a quiet man, but when he spoke, people listened.

"I don't know too much about a strike," said Alfred. "I never ever had anything to do with unioning before. But we ain't gonna let Skinner fire Jimmy and Russ without doin' something about it. Now if Skinner won't take them back — and you fellers all know Skinner, there ain't much chance he'll take them back — then either we got to strike or just give up, don't we?"

Andrew heard the men stirring and muttering. *That's right. Proper thing. Old Alfred hit 'er on the head.*

"Seems to me," said Alfred, "we ought to tell Skinner he's got to take them men back, and buy fish from Phonse, too. If he won't, then we're goin' on strike, and we're *stayin'* on strike till we get our union recognized."

Ambrose kept on objecting. So did Billy Morgan and some others. But most of the fisherman agreed with Alfred. When Jimmy Parker finally put it to a vote, only five hands were raised against the strike — and over sixty were in favour.

The next day was cold and raw, with low clouds skidding quickly overhead, and seagulls clawing their way up into the wind. At lunch time Andrew and Scott marched firmly down Water Street, heads bent against the wind, looking at the grey pavement.

"You know what I hate about this place?" Scott cried.

"What?"

"All this wind and fog and rain. You never see the sun in Widow's Harbour!"

"Makes it all the better when you do see it," yelled Andrew.

"You know, it's probably sunny at Spectacle Cove right now," said Scott. "That's not very far away."

"They say Widow's Harbour is where the fog is made," cried Andrew. "There's always fog along the shore, and Widow's Harbour sticks out so far in the ocean that we get fog lots of times when nobody else does."

"There's your dad!" said Scott. "And Buck and Jimmy. What are they doing?"

Andrew looked up. The three men were stamping their feet and talking in front of the big gates of the fish plant. The boys went running over.

"What's going on, Dad?"

"Skinner won't see us," said Phonse. "So we're gonna stop him when he drives out for to go home to lunch."

"That's him now, isn't it?" asked Buck, pointing at a blue sedan rolling towards the gate. It stopped inside, and Andrew saw Skinner's puzzled face behind the wheel. The men were standing at the side of the gate. He's going to roar right past them, Andrew thought. They aren't going to get to say a word to him.

As the gate opened, Skinner gunned the engine. Suddenly Andrew knew what to do. He stepped in front of the car, and Skinner screeched to a stop

before he had even really started. The car's front bumper was almost touching Andrew's knees.

"Good man, Andrew!" whispered Jimmy, coming around beside him. Buck opened the driver's door.

"I'm sorry to stop you," said Buck, "but I think you should know that the union members are pretty upset about what you did the other day."

"There's going to be more fired if there's any more union talk," said the manager. He blew his horn at Andrew and Jimmy. "Listen, you two, get out of my way! I'm late for lunch."

"We thought maybe you'd have changed your mind once you had a chance to think about it," Buck said.

"You've given me no reason to change my mind," snapped the manager. "I fired them, and they're staying fired." He blew the horn again.

"All right," said Buck, "but you ought to know the men are ready to go on strike over this."

"Go on strike, then!" cried the manager. "Go ahead! I don't need you. I can get fishermen anywhere. You'll be the ones to suffer." He eased the car forward until it was nudging Andrew and Jimmy. Buck waved at them, and they stepped aside. Skinner pulled ahead a short distance until he was abreast of Phonse.

"Goin' on strike, are you, Gurney?"

"Could be, " said Phonse.

"You'll be out until the snow flies," said Skinner.

"And you'll all come crawling back to me at the end of it, down on your hands and knees *begging* for a job."

Phonse shrugged, and the manager stepped on the gas. The big sedan shot down the street, swerving around potholes.

"Well, boys," said Jimmy cheerfully, rubbing his hands as he watched the car vanish around the corner, "looks like we're on strike!"

"Andy," said Buck, "you shouldn't have stepped in front of that car."

"Only way to stop him," Andrew protested.

"The way it worked out, I'm just as glad you did," said Buck. "But you could have got yourself hurt, even killed. We've got better things for you to do."

"Like what?"

"Come straight home after school," said Buck. "Bring Denny. Bring any of your friends. We've got some signs to paint."

"Sure!" said Andrew. "You comin', Scott?"

"Sure!"

The two boys were starting to run when Buck's voice stopped them.

"Andy? Scott?"

"Yeah?"

"What's that boy of Ambrose Hendsbee called? His nephew?"

"Ernie."

"Bring Ernie, will you? For sure?"

"What?" said Andrew.

"You heard me. Bring Ernie."

Andrew looked at Scott and raised his eyebrows.

"Okay, Buck. We'll bring him."

Down in the basement, Phonse's power saw screamed, and a pile of dark brown sawdust grew steadily under the saw table. Phonse was running pieces of hardboard through the saw, cutting them into sections. As each sheet was cut up, Andrew would pick it up and deliver it to Scott, Denny, and Ernie. The boys would paint the hardboard white. A few pieces were already dry, and Leo Gurney, Denny's father, was painting a message on one of them. *RECOGNIZE OUR UNION*, said the black letters on the white signboard.

Phonse finished the last piece of hardboard and began running some boards through the saw, cutting them into strips. When the signs were done, they could be nailed to the strips of wood and carried on a picket line. Buck came in from outside with some more boards.

"Give me a hand with these, will you, Andy?"

Andrew nodded and went outside with Buck.

"You were wondering why I wanted Ernie, weren't you?" Buck asked, picking up a couple of boards.

"Kind of."

"Because of Ambrose, " said Buck. "You notice how Ambrose isn't really involved with the union?

24

How he's always pulling us back? There's always a fellow like that."

"What's Ernie got to do with it?"

"Oh, well, if Ernie's involved, it's that much harder for Ambrose to stay out of it. If we get Ernie down here painting signs and all excited about the union, Ambrose is going to feel crummy about letting his nephew down."

"Uh-huh."

"You don't sound very convinced."

"I don't like Ernie very much."

"Why not?"

"He tells you one thing, and then he goes and does something else," said Andrew. "Like he says he's going to come and play hockey with you, and then he winds up fooling around with George Jackson's electric train. Anything you've got, he wants to use it. But you don't get to use anything of his."

"Selfish," said Buck.

"Yeah, sort of. He really likes to hang around with George. And Jeff Ritcey. They always got the best of everything. And right now they're dead set against the strike and the union and everything."

"Well, sure they are. George's father manages the bank, doesn't he? And Jeff Ritcey's old man is Ritcey's Stores, if I got it right?"

"Yeah."

"Well, they're bound to be opposed to the union. You can't spend much at a store with your strike pay. Maybe you can't meet your loan payments at the

25

bank. The whole town's going to slow right down as far as money is concerned, and those two men are going to feel it."

"I never thought about it," said Andrew.

"You bet they are. So they'll be working on people like Ambrose, and their sons are going to put the pressure on Ernie. If you can keep Ernie in with the union bunch, that might be one of the best things you could do for the union."

"Well, I can try," Andrew said.

"Andy," said Buck, "I'm sorry if I'm asking you to do something difficult."

"It's not that bad. It's just you can't trust him. Hey, Buck, what's Jimmy Parker doing in L'Anse au Griffon?"

"Organizing a strike," said Buck. "The union's got a man over there, too, and it's the same company owns that fish plant. So when the boys over there heard Widow's Harbour was on strike, they thought maybe they'd go out on strike, too."

"They're mostly all French over there," said Andrew. "Widow's Harbour's always against 'em in baseball and hockey and everything."

"Well, this time you're on the same side. If they don't strike, we can't win."

"How come?"

"Because the company can just bring its boats in over there and put the fish through that plant instead of this one. It wouldn't bother them very much if this plant stayed shut down forever. They'd still make money."

"Andrew!" called Phonse from the cellar door. "Oh, sorry, Buck. Listen, I'm out of boards. You fellers bringing some, or not?"

"Coming," said Buck, laughing. They carried some boards inside, and Andrew walked across the basement to where the boys were painting. Scott was slowest of them all, carefully covering his panels with white. Leo, Scott, and Denny were shouting at one another, grinning. Ernie stood silent, carefully dipping his brush in the paint and filling in the letters.

Phonse finished ripping up the boards, and the saw fell silent.

"Phonse, Leo," said Buck. "We got a letter to write. Maybe we should go in and write it. The boys can finish the signs, can't you?"

"Sure," said Andrew. The others all nodded.

Leo straightened up with a groan.

"Suits me," he said. "I ain't used to this fiddling work."

"Come on, Ernie," said Andrew. "Let's you and me do the lettering and let them do the white."

"Okay," said Ernie.

The afternoon settled into an easy working rhythm. Ernie was really good at lettering, Andrew noticed, and after a few messy jobs Ernie worked out a whole new system. He ruled off two lines on a piece of cardboard, and he printed his letters between the lines. Then he cut the letters out, ruled two lines on the signboard, traced the letters between the lines, and filled in the tracing with black paint.

"That's really neat!" said Andrew, when he saw what Ernie was up to.

"Like it?"

"It looks like a real sign painter did it."

Ernie said nothing, but he smiled. The boys worked on, chatting about people they knew, about boats, about books.

"You read *The Phantom Freighter* yet?" Andrew asked Scott.

"Nope."

"It's one of the best Hardy Boys."

"I seen them on TV," said Ernie. "Didn't like them."

"The books are better," said Scott. "I wouldn't mind being the Hardy boys, eh, Andrew?"

"Yeah," said Andrew, squinting at his sign. "Trouble is, you never get mysteries around here. Nobody ever does anything."

"Gonna be enough excitement in this strike," grunted Denny.

"Too much excitement," said Ernie. "You can't fight the company."

"Well, you can't just lay down and let 'em kick you!" said Denny.

"Not the same thing, anyway," Andrew interjected. "You want to catch people doing stuff — stealing things, or smuggling, stuff like that."

"I'd sooner chase after fish in a dragger," grinned Denny. "Anyway, everybody and his dog's going to be chasin' after us if this strike goes on very long."

"That's right," said Ernie fiercely.

Denny looked at Ernie.

"Those guys bugged you pretty bad today, didn't they?"

"Bad enough," said Ernie.

"What's all this?" Andrew asked.

"George Jackson and Jeff Ritcey and them," Denny explained. "They give Ernie a pretty bad time today. Called him a little wharf rat and stuff. They went off to play pool at George's place and wouldn't let him come along. Some nice friends you got there, Ernie."

"They're not my friends." said Ernie. He kept his face low and his voice wavered. "I always thought they were but they ain't."

"What made 'em change?" asked Scott.

"The strike, you dummy," said Denny. "They were runnin' down the fishermen. Said they were stupid, pig-ignorant, said they were out to ruin the town. Ernie said no, and they just turned right on him. Right, Ernie?"

Ernie said nothing.

"You're a fisherman's boy," Denny said. "And they're against the fishermen. You won't be seein' too much of them for a while."

Ernie said nothing. His head nodded.

At lunch time the next day, Phonse was among the

men walking back and forth in front of the plant, carrying the signs. *CONSOLIDATED FISHERIES UNFAIR TO FISHERMEN. RECOGNIZE OUR UNION. ALLIED FISHERMEN'S UNION ON STRIKE.*

"Took a letter to Skinner this morning," Phonse told his son when Andrew stopped by on his way home for lunch. "It said until they hire our men back and recognize our union, the fishermen are on strike. Look over at the wharf, there."

Andrew looked where he pointed.

"Four boats tied up. There's four more at sea, and they'll tie up when they get in. No more fish after that."

A tall man in a soiled white apron came up to Russ Ryan, who was marching back and forth in front of the gate with a sign. Andrew knew the man a little bit. He was Russ's cousin, and he worked in the plant, cutting fish.

"No more work today, I guess," said the tall man. "We ain't gonna cross that picket line to go back after lunch. You fellers plan on picketing for a good while, I guess?"

"Yeah, till Skinner changes his mind," said Russ.

"Good enough," said the plant worker. "This time tomorrow that plant is gonna be shut right down."

"Well, that's A-1," said Russ.

"We're union men in the plant, you know," said the tall man. "No way we're gonna break your picket line."

After school the men were still there. Father Guthrie was talking with some of them. If the fishermen wanted to make themselves a cup of tea, or get out of the rain or anything, he said, the basement of the rectory would always be open. They could go in there whenever they wanted.

"That's kind of you, Father."

"Wish all the preachers felt that way."

Father Guthrie wanted to know what the other priests and ministers had been doing.

"They ain't doin' much, Father, but some of them won't speak to a fisherman any more."

"One of them turned and went around the block rather than pass by the picket line."

That night Andrew woke up from a sound sleep, feeling thirsty. He walked down the creaking old stairs and out into the kitchen. Phonse was having a cup of tea and listening to the news and weather on the radio, the way he did every night. If the weather was going to be stormy, the fishermen wouldn't go out.

"In Widow's Harbour," said the radio, "striking fishermen have idled the fish plant, the town's only industry. The fishermen have said they'll keep their picket lines up until the company agrees to recognize their union, the Allied Fishermen of Canada. Reports from L'Anse au Griffon say that union fishermen there have closed the other plant owned by Consolidated Fisheries in sympathy with the Widow's Harbour fishermen. One of the Widow's Harbour

fishermen spoke with CFXY's reporter, Frank
Helliwell—"

And then came a voice that Andrew recognized
very well.

"We ain't gonna back down," said the voice. "We
give the company the chance to avoid this strike, but
they didn't take it. All we want is a union, same as any
other working man's got, and we're gonna stay out
here on the road till we get it."

"Dad!" shouted Andrew. "That's *you* on the radio!"

"Yeas, it is," grinned Phonse. "Feller came down on
the picket line today with a tape recorder, wanted to
talk to someone about the strike. Sure, I'll talk, I said,
and the other fellers agreed, so I did."

Andrew was really excited. Nobody he knew had
ever been on the news before.

Soon the strike settled into a routine. Every day the
fishermen walked the picket line while the plant and
the boats stood empty and silent. Farm trucks
rumbled into Widow's Harbour, heaped high with
potatoes and turnips sent by the Farmers' Union to
help feed the families. Other unions were sending
money—the electrical workers in Toronto, the
miners in Sudbury, the garbage collectors in Halifax, the steelworkers in Sydney, the fishermen in
British Columbia. Andrew's mother offered to keep
track of the money, and Andrew worked along with
her. Laura marked down each donation, bundled the
cheques up, and sent Andrew to the bank with them.

She wrote out cheques to pay for printing leaflets, for gas for the cars when the men had to go away for meetings, for strike pay to keep the families eating. Every Saturday the striking fishermen would stop by the house, and Andrew would pass them each a cheque for a few dollars. It was all the union could afford to give them.

After school the boys often stopped by the picket line. The men had rigged up an old stove in Father Guthrie's basement, because the weather could be cold and raw even in June, and while some of the men walked the picket line with their signs, the others would gather around the stove and talk.

"Skinner's tryin' to starve us out."

"Let him try. You can't starve a fisherman. A steelworker, yes, an auto worker, yes. But not a farmer, not a fisherman."

"That right. We're always gonna eat. And people need food. Someone's gonna buy that fish."

"You fellers know the government pretty well owns this fish plant? Government loaned 'em four million dollars to build her, and they ain't paid back a cent yet. Say they ain't makin' any money."

"Go on."

Buck kept his guitar in the rectory basement, and sometimes he would get it out and play and sing. Over the long days of picketing, the fishermen taught him some of their own songs, songs of the Atlantic Coast, and when he sang those, they would all join in:

Oh doctor, oh doctor, oh doctor dear John,
Your cod-liver oil is so pure and so strong;
I'm afraid for me life, I'll go down in the soil,
If me wife don't stop drinkin' your cod-liver oil.

Roaring it out, the men would fairly make the windows rattle, and Scott told Andrew he could feel the floor vibrating under his feet while he did his homework. And then Buck would teach the fishermen some union songs. Before long, they were roaring those out, too:

Oh, workers, can you stand it?
Tell me how you can!
Will you be a lousy scab
Or will you be a man?

"What's a scab, Buck?" Denny asked.

"Someone who goes to work in the place of a person on strike," Buck said. "If I was to go fishing for the company now, while the regular fishermen are on strike, then I'd be a scab."

"Will the company get scabs?" asked Andrew.

"Maybe," said Buck. "You never know. Here, you sing now."

Andrew took the guitar, feeling rather shy. Buck was teaching him how to play, but he wasn't good at it yet. He loved it all the same, the big awkward body of the guitar purring against him, the clear chiming of the strings. He sang:

I know a man by the name of Skinner,
Hey lilee, lilee lo;

Got so mad it spoiled his dinner,
Hey lilee, lilee lo.

That was his favourite of all Buck's songs, because you could make it up as you went along, and fit anyone into it.

This here's Denny, he's my cousin,
Hey lilee, lilee lo;
I got cousins by the dozens,
Hey lilee, lilee lo.

Then everyone could join in and sing *Hey lilee, lilee lo* a few times for a chorus, and the leader would continue:

Boys, I'll tell you what I wish,
Hey lilee, lilee lo;
Decent price for a pound of fish,
Hey lilee, lilee lo.

They could go on all afternoon.

3

SCHOOL ended for the summer. The strike had been going on for six weeks and it seemed to be taking up more and more time. Louis Bond and Charlie Johnston went up to Sudbury to talk to the miners' union there, and to the workers in the nickel refinery. They went on down to Toronto and talked to electrical workers and to the postal workers and store clerks. They talked to the steelworkers in Hamilton, and to the automobile workers in Oshawa. The men on the picket line listened to radio reports about Louis and Charlie, and shook their heads.

"Think of old Louis givin' a speech. Never thought I'd see it."

"Five hundred people, they said?" asked Billy Morgan.

"Six hundred. And they passed the hat and collected — how much, Andrew?" Russ asked.

"Eight hundred and seventy dollars," said Andrew. "Mom got the money order this morning."

"Lot of money."

"Not when you think it's a hundred and fifty families between here and L'Anse au Griffon," said Ambrose Hendsbee. "About five bucks a family, that's all it is."

The fishermen and their families got used to reporters coming down with notepads and tape recorders, then printing their stories in the papers, or reading them on the radio. Again and again Buck explained that two things could end the strike. Either the company could agree to bargain with the fishermen, or the government could give fishermen the same right to a union that other workers had, and then the company would *have* to bargain with them.

"Why do you think the government hasn't acted?" asked a young woman, holding a microphone up to Buck's mouth.

"Because there are an awful lot of fishermen in Nova Scotia," Buck said. "When we get them all into a union, the companies are going to have to treat them properly, and the government is going to have to listen to them. In other words, the companies and the government are going to have a little less power. Well, nobody gives up power if they don't have to."

On a bright, breezy day, Scott waded into the water beside Phonse's little private wharf. Andrew,

Denny, and Ernie watched him closely. Scott was wearing his new wetsuit and face mask, with a rubber snorkel sticking up behind his head, and flat, awkward flippers on his feet.

"Cold!" he gasped as the water filtered into his wetsuit. Then, after a minute, "It's warming up now."

He lay down on his face in the water and kicked away from shore. They could hear him breathing heavily through the snorkel. He seemed to be lying almost on top of the water, hardly sinking into it at all.

"Guess that rubber suit holds him up," said Andrew.

Scott turned and swam back towards the shore. With his flippers he moved very quickly through the water. Near the beach, he stood up.

"It's really nice," he called, pulling the snorkel out of his mouth. "The water's really clear. I can see little fish all over the place."

"Is it cold?" asked Ernie.

"Not now," said Scott. "Just at first."

"Wish I could try it," said Ernie.

"You can try it," said Scott. "All of you can try it. But we need a little more time, more than we have today."

"We should take a whole day," said Ernie.

"We were going to go for clams," Denny pointed out.

"How about that?" said Andrew. "Out on the outside of Spaniard's Island?"

"Yeah!" said Ernie excitedly. "Go in the morning and stay all day."

"When?" said Scott.

"Can't go tomorrow," said Denny. "Andrew 'n' me, we promised to help the old man dig up the cellar drain."

"First fine day after that?" Andrew suggested.

"Good enough," said Denny. "Must be almost supper time now, isn't it?"

"I want to go in once more," Scott said quickly. "I want some weight, I'm going to try going down deeper."

Andrew looked around.

"Here's an old anchor."

"Put a bit of rope on it and throw it over," said Scott. "I can pull myself down the rope."

Andrew scrounged inside his father's gear shed, found some rope and tied it to the anchor.

"Sling it as far out as you can," Scott said.

Denny took the anchor, swung it back and forth and let it fly out into the calm waters of the Tiddle. Scott flopped back into the water and swam out to the anchor rope. He nodded at them and pulled himself down the rope in a swirl of water and bubbles.

"Must be neat down there," said Ernie.

"Like to see it myself," said Andrew.

"That a boat coming this way?" asked Denny.

The three boys listened. They could all hear it: the high-pitched whine of an outboard motor, growing rapidly louder.

"Hope he keeps clear of us, with Scott down there," said Andrew worriedly.

The water swirled again, and Scott's head bobbed out of the water. At the same moment, a speedboat came skimming around the rocks at the mouth of the Tiddle, and roared up the narrow strip of water among the moored boats and little wharves, like a crazy driver speeding down the main street of a village.

"Look out!"

"Slow down!"

"Watch out!"

The three boys on the wharf were all shouting at Scott and waving at the boat, trying to show the speedboat where Scott was bobbing in the water. But the speedboat kept right on coming, heading directly at Scott. Andrew suddenly realized that the driver couldn't see Scott at all, with the sun low over the water and shining directly in his eyes.

Andrew jumped.

He felt himself flying through the air, hoping the speedboat would see him against the sky, and then he dropped with a great splash into the water, almost on top of Scott. He was tumbling underwater, with the sound of the engine beating hard against his ears, and then it faded and slowed down, and as his head came to the surface he saw the speedboat dead in the water a stone's throw away, and the horrified face of Jeff Ritcey's father looking at the two boys he had nearly run down.

Denny was standing at the end of the wharf screeching at Frank Ritcey. As Andrew and Scott paddled to the shore, they made out a few words — "maniac...foolishness...look where you're going..."

"No harm done!" snapped Ritcey angrily, and he gunned his motor, made a quick circle in the water and raced down the Tiddle and back out into the main harbour again.

"You all right?" Andrew asked, feeling the water dripping off him.

"Yeah. You?" Scott asked.

"Didn't look, couldn't see, just roared down in here like a crazy man!" Denny snapped. "Guy like that shouldn't have a boat!"

"He was only this far away when he turned!" marvelled Ernie, holding his arms outstretched.

"Father like that, it's no wonder Jeff's such a pain in the neck!" Denny exclaimed. "Hasn't got the brains God gave to geese. None of them Ritceys got anything under their hair at all!"

"Jeff's not too bad," said Ernie, nervously.

"You can't trust Jeff no farther than you can throw him!" raged Denny. "Look at the way he turned on you, just because your uncle's in the union!"

"Yeah, but —"

"But nothin'! You ever play hockey with him? Yeah, and he's all tripping and butt-ending with his stick? You ever see him do anything he promised, unless there's something in it for Jeff?"

"I'm freezing," shivered Andrew. "Come on,

Denny, let's go."

Scott had his mask and flippers off, and Andrew's clothes were clinging to him like plastic wrapping paper. Squelching and dripping, the two of them led the way.

"What happened there, anyway?" Scott asked as they walked along the side of the wharf.

"He couldn't see you," Andrew explained. "Sun in his eyes. I couldn't think of anything else to make him slow down and sheer off, so I jumped in, too."

"Wow! You mean he'd have hit me?"

"Looked like it."

They stepped onto the road leading to the rectory, at the bottom of a steep little hill. Andrew looked down at the trail of water on the pavement.

"You saved my life, Andrew!"

"Nah, likely he would've seen you."

Two bicycles came flying over the hill and raced down at them.

"Look out!" cried Denny.

Trying to run, Ernie stumbled heavily into Denny, and both of them fell down. George Jackson and Jeff Ritcey were coming right at them with their bicycles, and they swerved hard trying to miss the two fallen boys. George's bicycle slipped out from under him, and both the boy and the bike skidded and bounced on the road. The bike smashed into Denny. Denny cried out.

"Look at my bike!" cried George.

Denny was breathing heavily, trying not to cry. A thick gout of blood welled out of his forehead.

George's yellow bike was all scratched and scraped.

"That's a brand-new bike, you moron!" shouted George.

"Never mind your bike!" snapped Andrew. "Look at his head!"

"Teach him to get out of the way!" George roared.

"Teach you to watch where you're going!" Andrew yelled.

George took a step forward, swung his fist back, and punched Andrew hard in the face. It made Andrew's head ring, but before he knew what was happening he had already waded into George, hitting him hard in the body. He felt George hit him again, and he hooked a foot behind George's leg and pushed against George's chest. George fell backwards with Andrew on top of him. Andrew felt Jeff kick him in the side, and then he felt Scott's wet diving suit skidding over his face. Then he was alone on top of George again, with George wriggling furiously. George reached up, grabbed Andrew's throat, and squeezed. Andrew felt his wind going and tore George's hand away. George punched him with the other hand and heaved with his body. Andrew went sprawling on the road. He felt George land on him, and then someone blew a horn.

George let go. Andrew looked up. Scott and Denny were getting up off Jeff, and George was struggling to his feet. Skinner's car was parked beside them, and Skinner was scowling out the window.

"You Gurneys!" scolded Skinner. "Three against two! Leave those boys alone."

"They started it," said Andrew.

"Don't give me your sauce," said the manager. "Jeff and George, run along. I'll stay here till you're gone."

"They've wrecked my new bike," said George sullenly.

"I don't doubt it," said Skinner. "You'd better go."

George and Jeff picked up their bikes, dusted themselves off, and rode away.

"Young Guthrie, you can be sure your father is going to hear about this," said Skinner. "A priest's son, brawling in the road!"

"They ran into us!" said Scott indignantly. "Look at Denny's face! They did that with the bike!"

"So you had to ruin their bikes and beat them up, eh?" said Skinner. "The Gurneys don't know any better, but you do."

"You don't —" Scott began, but the manager rolled up his car window and drove away.

Andrew looked at Scott. His new diving suit was all dirty and it had a rip in one elbow. Denny's face was streaked with blood and dust. And Ernie —

"Hey, where's Ernie?"

All three of them looked around. Ernie was nowhere to be seen.

"We better go get cleaned up," said Denny.

"That Skinner!" said Andrew. "Wouldn't listen at all."

They started on towards the rectory. When they got to the corner, Ernie came running towards them.

"I went to get some help!" he puffed.

Denny looked at him with a level gaze.

"We didn't need no help," he said. "Except from Ernie Hendsbee."

"Well, I thought — George is pretty big —"

"Sure he is. And Jeff ain't too bad, ain't that what you said?"

"Leave him alone, Denny," said Andrew. "It all worked out all right."

Two days later Andrew was walking with Scott and Denny down to the picket line. Scott had his diving gear in a bag. The summer grass was high and green, and they could hear crickets chirping all around them. The little painted houses of Widow's Harbour looked as though they had been thrown down along the rocky harbour by a careless giant. Ahead of them the bulky white fish plant was giving off waves of heat under the sun. In front of it Phonse, Paul Nickerson, and Freddy Quinn were holding signs and walking back and forth, back and forth, from one end of the plant to the other.

"Ernie coming today?" asked Denny.

"No answer at his place," said Andrew. "I called a couple of times."

"He really wanted to come with us," Scott said.

"Must be around town somewheres," said Denny.

They came up to the picket line. Phonse reached over and ran his hand through Andrew's hair.

"Lo, boys," Freddy nodded. "How's she goin'?"

"Can't complain," Denny said. "How's your hand?"

Freddy looked down at his left hand. His one finger

and his thumb stuck out from a grey wad of band-ages.

"Don't hurt too much now," he said. "Tell you the truth, though, I did like that hand a whole lot better with five fingers."

"Well, I imagine!" said Denny.

Phonse turned to Andrew.

"Ain't seen too much of you lately. What you been up to?"

"Mom put me to weedin' that garden," Andrew said. "I hate that, grubbin' away in the dirt."

"You like eatin', though," said Phonse. "These days, you can't have the one without you have the other."

"Don't mind diggin' clams," said Andrew. "You seen Ernie, Dad? He was gonna come with us."

"Ernie was here," said Paul. "Look, ain't that him down by the oil tanks, on the bike there?"

Scott waved, and Ernie turned the bike and rode swiftly towards them.

"Wonder when the strike's going to be over," Denny said.

"No way to tell," said Phonse, turning with the others for another walk past the plant. "Skinner don't seem to be in any rush to back down, but then the only one that really knows what Skinner's thinking is Skinner."

Ernie pulled up while Phonse was speaking. Now he looked up at Andrew's father.

"He was over to Ritcey's the other night," said Ernie. "He said you'd be walkin' the picket line till

46

you had whiskers down to your knees, far as he was concerned."

"Could be just sayin' that," said Phonse. "He wants to get us discouraged, but we ain't goin' to. Wish we had a little more money, though. Some of the fellers find it hard going, trying to keep a family on twenty bucks a week."

"They don't always *get* twenty bucks," said Andrew. "It's all according to what comes in."

"Well, we're gonna have a fish sale," said Phonse. "That might help some. And there's more people writing in and sending a little money all the time. We'll manage."

Ambrose Hendsbee came down the road towards them, ready to take his turn walking the picket line.

"Ernie, I thought I told you to stay home," said Ambrose grumpily.

"Hello, Ambrose," said Phonse. "Just talkin' about the strike pay."

"Can't keep up the strike if we don't get some more," said Ambrose. "I hear a lot of grumblin' these days."

Phonse turned to the boys.

"Weren't you fellers goin' to dig some clams?"

"Yeah, we were," said Andrew. "We want to take the dory and go over outside of Spaniard's Island."

"Sure," said Phonse. "Take the dory and run along."

"That don't include you, Ernie," said Ambrose quickly. "Now git."

"But I —" said Ernie.

"But we —" Scott began.

"Just git," said Ambrose. Ernie shot a fierce look at his uncle, then turned his bike and pedalled furiously away. The other boys just looked at Ambrose. Phonse, standing behind Ambrose, raised his eyebrows and nodded his head sideways.

"See you," said Andrew unhappily. When the three of them were out of hearing, he burst out, "That ain't fair!"

"Poor old Ernie," said Scott. "It was his idea, too, going out for the whole day."

"That Ambrose," said Denny shaking his head.

The boys rowed the dory around the tip of Spaniard's Island and landed facing the open sea. The tide was low and the dory crunched onto the coarse sand a long way from the island itself.

Denny jumped ashore with a small rusty anchor and walked as far up the beach as the rope would allow. He stuck the anchor firmly into the sand so that the dory couldn't float away if the tide should happen to come up again before they got back to the boat.

"Tides are tricky," Denny told Scott. "But you got to dig clams at low tide. The part of the beach where they live is all covered with water at high tide."

"How do you dig them?" asked Scott.

"Come on with me," said Andrew. "I'll show you."

"I'll dig right here," said Denny.

"All right," said Andrew. "We'll go this way."

Andrew and Scott walked down the beach until they came to a place where the sand was full of neat round holes, as though someone had been shooting a rifle down from the sky into the beach.

"Good spot," said Andrew. "Now you try and dig right down fast, get 'em up before they can get away. Clams can go down awful fast, sometimes. Faster than you can dig." He drove his shovel down into the beach and spread the sand out. Among the rocks and gravel were three white clams.

"Pop them in the bucket," said Andrew. He dug a few more and then let Scott have a try. When he could see Scott had the idea, he took a bucket and a shovel and went on down the beach to another likely spot.

It was a good beach, Andrew thought, turning over another shovelful, and noticing that his bucket was already half full. When he had filled it, he was sweating. He looked up and saw that Denny was sitting down, while Scott was still working. On his way back to the dory, he stopped at Scott's side.

"You're doing fine." Scott's bucket was almost full. Andrew set down his bucket and turned over a few shovelfuls. They picked up their shovels and buckets and went to join Denny.

"How come it's called Spaniard's Island?" asked Scott.

"Spanish ship got wrecked here one time. Just over there," said Denny, lifting his head and pointing.

"When was that?"

"Dunno," murmured Denny. "Long time ago, any-ways."

"Two hundred years or so," said Andrew lazily, lying down on the sand. "S'posed to be loaded with treasure. That's why they call it Gold Point."

"Hey," said Scott excitedly, "Anybody ever go diving for it?"

"Not that I know," said Andrew. Suddenly he was wide awake. He could see what Scott was driving at. "You mean *you* could go diving for it?"

"Yeah!" said Scott. "With the wetsuit and every-thing —"

"Holy snappin'," said Denny. "No harm tryin', any-ways."

"Come on!" cried Scott. "Let's have a look at Gold Point!"

They loaded the clams and the tools into the dory and rowed over to the nearby point. The point itself was wooded and ended in a raw, red bluff of naked earth. From there on the point thrust out into the water in the form of great rocks and boulders. As Andrew rowed out from the point, the others could see the bottom slowly dropping away beneath them.

"That point is washing away all the time," said Denny.

"How much?" asked Scott.

"Little bit every year," said Denny.

"Holy cow," said Scott. "If that ship went down 200

years ago, the point was a lot longer. Listen, let's go back in and get a couple of rocks."

"Why?" asked Andrew.

"To make me sink," said Scott. "If we use a rock on a rope, I can just hang onto the rock and go down with it. I have to get suited up, anyway."

Andrew turned the dory around and rowed towards the shore. Did they really have a chance of finding Spanish gold, he wondered. He could get a bike. Or even a speedboat like Ritcey's. Or diving stuff of his own. Maybe — just maybe —!

Scott changed right on the beach and clambered back aboard with his flippers in one hand and a big net bag in his other hand. "Need something to carry whatever we find," he explained. Denny had found a big rock and tied the end of the anchor line around it. They shoved off again and rowed far out on the reef that stuck out from Gold Point.

Scott peered over the side. "Let's try here," he said. He let himself over the stern of the dory, gasped as the cold water seeped inside his wetsuit, and pulled his mask over his face.

"Okay," he said, "give me that rock."

Denny held the rock over the stern of the dory. Scott grabbed the rope just above the rock.

"When I nod, let it go," he said. He took two or three deep breaths, then nodded. Denny released the rope, and Scott flipped over in the water. His flippers broke the surface, and then all they could see was a cloud of bubbles. As the bubbles cleared, they could see Scott on the bottom, still holding onto the rope, looking around. A cloud of bubbles came out of his snorkel. Then he let go of the rope and shot up to the surface again.

"Can't see much," he said. "Haul that rock up."

They hauled up the rock, moved the dory a little further out, and Scott plunged to the bottom again. The water was deeper, and it was hard to see his black form against the dark bottom. Suddenly he was rising again. He broke water beside the boat.

"What kind of clams live on the sand?" he said.

"Clams?"

"Maybe they're not clams. They look like big round clams, as big as your hand. They can move, too."

"Scallops!" said Andrew. "Those are scallops!"

"Are they good to eat?"

"Are they ever!" said Andrew. "Can you get a bunch?"

"Sure," said Scott. "When I nod, let 'er go."

When he broke the surface again, Scott had five scallops.

"Wish I had tanks," he gasped. "I can't stay down very long just holding my breath. If I had tanks I could stay down for an hour."

"You're doing fine," said Denny. "Any more scallops down there?"

"Lots of them," said Scott. He breathed deeply, nodded, and dived again. After three or four dives he had a bulging bag of scallops. And he was tired.

Denny grabbed his arms, and Andrew grabbed his feet. Moving very carefully so as not to upset the dory, they pulled him aboard.

"Denny, you want to try the suit?" he puffed.

"Not me. I can't swim."

"You try it, Andrew. Go ahead."

"You don't mind?"

"I want to find out what's down there," Scott said, with determination. "Go ahead and try it."

They rowed ashore. The suit was really tight, but Andrew finally got it on. Scott gave him the mask and snorkel, and Andrew padded about near the shore. It was amazing how well he could see underwater, and how big things looked. His hand seemed enormous.

They rowed out to a different part of the reef, and Andrew let himself gently over the side. After the first shock, he could feel the water warming up inside the suit. Soon it was just like wearing a wet, warm second skin.

"Take a good breath," said Scott, "and then just let the rock take you down. When it feels like your lungs are bursting, let go. You can breathe out a little bit on the way up."

"Okay," said Andrew. "I'll try it."

He took the rope tied to the rock, took a deep breath, and nodded. Denny let the rock go, and he felt it pulling his arm down. Then he was rushing down, down, with the bottom coming up at him. He looked around him, at the fronds of seaweed waving like grass in a slow, slow breeze. A fish about as long as his hand darted out of a hole in the rocks and shot into the grass. He could hardly believe how fast it seemed to move. He looked over the jumbled rocks beside the grass and saw a pop can. He let go of the rope, feeling his lungs straining for air, and reached for the can. Before he could touch it, he was racing up to the silvery roof above him. He could see the bottom of the dory coming faster and faster, and then suddenly his head burst out into the sunlight and he was breathing hard.

"It's — really — neat!" he said, treading water slowly.

He made another dive, then another and another, exploring this wet miniature jungle. But he saw nothing that looked like Spanish gold, and he could feel himself getting cold and tired. When he reached the surface, he could feel himself shaking.

"Better quit," said Scott.

"Just once more," said Andrew. He took a deep breath and nodded at Denny. Denny dropped the rock, and again Andrew was pulled down towards the browns and greens and yellows of the ocean floor. The dory had drifted, and they were over the edge of the reef. On one side he could see the rocky jumble rising above him, and on the other side a dark green space where the water suddenly dropped away from the reef. One of the rocks not far away looked strange. It was completely round, where the others were rough and jagged, and — it wasn't a rock. It was a

54

bowl, all overgrown with seaweed, lying upside down among the boulders. He could feel himself running out of air, but he gave a desperate wriggle and touched the bowl, another wriggle and caught it by the rim. Then, with his chest feeling as though it were going to explode, he let go of the rope and felt himself rising quickly towards the surface, the bowl clutched tightly in his hand.

Wordlessly he held the bowl over the side of the dory. Denny took it aboard.

"A bowl!" said Scott unhappily. "Here I thought you really had something!"

"Best thing we've seen, except the scallops," said Denny.

"Pull — me — aboard," puffed Andrew.

They pulled him over the side, and he lay gasping in the bottom of the dory. Denny rowed for shore while Scott looked over the pottery bowl. Scraping away the seaweed, he could make out that it was pale green inside and reddish outside, like a flower pot. The rim of it had a piece broken out of it, and a long crack ran down one side.

"Some treasure," said Scott. "We should throw it back."

"Hey!" said Denny. "Andrew found it. If he wants it, he keeps it."

"It's all his," said Scott disappointedly.

Back on the beach, Andrew dried himself and got back into his jeans and his shirt. He was still shivering, but he could feel the warmth spreading through him again. He thought he heard something, listened, and felt sure.

"There's an outboard coming this way," he said. Scott and Denny listened. Sure enough, the sound grew stronger. Then Ritcey's speedboat shot out around the end of the island, made a big arc in the water, and headed straight for them.

"Not *them* again!" said Scott.

Jeff Ritcey cut the throttle near the beach, and the speedboat mushed down in the water and coasted heavily to the shore. George Jackson jumped out and hauled it up the beach. Then he peered inside the dory. He picked up a bucket of clams and dumped it out in the shallow water while Jeff Ritcey and Peter Thorpe laughed and got out behind him.

"Hey!" shouted Andrew, running down the beach. "You leave them clams alone!"

George laughed again and dumped another bucket out. Andrew went to grab him, but Peter and Jeff seized him and started punching him. Denny went flying around the struggling group, spun George around as he reached for the third bucket, and pushed him over into the water, then fell on top of him. Scott caught Peter by the neck and made him let go of Andrew. The six boys fought furiously. They were evenly matched, but Denny soon had George backing up the beach. Jeff gave Andrew a shove and scrambled after George. Scott was getting the worst of it with Peter, so Andrew grabbed Peter from behind and threw him on the ground.

Suddenly he saw a chance. He pushed quickly on the speedboat, which floated off. Scott was sitting on Peter, pounding him with his fists, and Denny was holding his own with the other two.

"Scott! Denny!"

They looked up when he called, saw what he was at, and ran for the dory with George and Jeff hard on Denny's heels. Suddenly Denny stopped, and they ran into him. George fell down, and Andrew tripped Jeff. Denny and Andrew jumped in the dory, and Scott shoved off. Jeff came floundering into the water after them. Scott swung an oar at him, and while Jeff ducked Andrew shoved off again with the other oar. They were clear of the beach, in deep enough water that the boys on shore couldn't reach them.

George picked up a rock and threw it. It hit the side of the dory with a sharp thump. Scott ducked. Andrew pushed him down and began to row. All three boys were throwing rocks now. Denny was shouting at them.

"Get down, Denny!" cried Andrew. A rock came flying at him and hit his knuckles. He cried out, but kept rowing. A few strokes took them out of range.

"That bunch!" choked Denny, filled with rage.

"They're stranded!" cried Scott gleefully.

"Not for long," said Andrew, pointing at the speedboat. It was slowly drifting towards the tip of Gold Point. Before long it would be close enough for the three on the shore to reach.

"We should go get it," said Denny. "Leave them stinkers there all night."

"We'd have to go too close," Andrew pointed out. He started rowing steadily for home. "They won't get it for a bit yet. By the time they do, we'll be home."

Scott was feeling his forehead. He had a big lump there, and an angry purple bruise was forming on it. "That hurts," he said.

"Bet it does," said Denny. "Dumped two buckets of clams, them three did."

"Scallops are better eatin', anyway," said Andrew.

"And we've still got Andrew's bowl," said Scott. The dory pulled around the corner of the island. The three boys on the beach still had not reached their speedboat. As he watched, Andrew saw one of them stripping off his clothes.

"They're going to swim for it," he said. "Let's get out of here. Come on, Denny."

Denny slipped in beside him. Each of them took an oar, and the dory picked up speed as their oars bit the water. Andrew was thinking to himself about something that had been eating away at his mind for the last few minutes.

"Scott," he said between strokes, "how come those fellers came around there?"

"I don't know."

"Went right to the — right place," said Andrew. "They weren't — just cruisin' around."

"That's right," said Denny. Andrew glanced over

his shoulder. They were almost to the Tiddle. In the distance he heard the outboard starting up. Could they make it to the wharf before the speedboat caught them? He gave an extra hard pull to his oar.

"Everybody knew we were out there," said Scott thoughtfully.

"Not everybody," said Andrew. "Only our families, and — the fellows on the picket line."

The speedboat came racing around the island, its tall rooster tail white against the dark blue water. Denny and Andrew rowed furiously. The dory nosed up to the government wharf, and Denny caught the rung of a ladder.

"Someone else knew," said Scott.

"Who?" Denny asked.

The speedboat came roaring around the end of the wharf, cut in viciously close to the dory, did a circle and raced away again. Denny shook a fist at it. Andrew was laughing.

"Those fellers look like they were in a fight, don't they?" said Andrew. "All wet and covered with sand —!"

"Some owly-lookin', too," said Denny grinning.

"Not happy at all," laughed Andrew. Denny jumped up on the wharf, and Scott handed up the diving gear. Andrew passed him the bucket of clams, and Scott lifted the bag of scallops.

"What about your bowl?" asked Scott.

"Might's well keep it," Andrew shrugged. "Souvenir, anyways. First time I ever went diving." He took the bowl under his arm and climbed up the ladder with Scott close behind him. They walked up the wharf towards the rectory, sweating in the sun.

"You said someone else knew we were out there," said Denny.

"Yeah."

"Who?"

"Ernie," said Scott.

"Hey, that's right," said Andrew.

"That son of a rubber boot!" said Denny. "Wait till I get my hands on him!"

"We don't know anything, really," said Scott cautiously. "But he did know we were going out there."

"Leave him be," said Andrew. "Let's see what happens. But it looks funny to me." They walked up the steps of the rectory and onto the back porch, setting down their gear.

"I'm hungry," said Scott. He pushed open the back door, and called, "Mom! Anything to eat?"

"She's out," came Father Guthrie's voice from another room. They heard footsteps, and then Father Guthrie appeared.

"How'd it go?"

"Not bad," said Scott. "Hey, there's some bananas."

"What happened to your face, son?" asked Father Guthrie. "Here, let me see that. That's quite a bruise."

"Had a little tangle with George Jackson and them," said Denny.

"What, over on the island?"

"Yeah," said Scott. "Don't touch it, Dad, it hurts!"

"What were they doing over there?"

"Don't know," said Andrew. "Bugging us, mostly."

"Look here," said Father Guthrie, sitting down at the kitchen table, "I think you'd better tell me exactly what happened."

They told him, and he was quietly angry at first, and then laughing when they described how they marooned the others on the island. But in the end he was more angry than amused.

"A little tussle on the beach is one thing," he said, "but they were really out to hurt you. And throwing rocks like that — they could have done some real damage. I'm going to talk with Frank Ritcey about this."

"Won't make no difference," said Denny.

"We'll see," said Father Guthrie. "So all the treasure you got was bumps and bruises, was it?"

"Got some scallops," said Denny.

"And I got an old bowl off the bottom," said Andrew. "Not much of a treasure, though."

"Let's see it," said Father Guthrie. Andrew went out to the porch and brought in the bowl.

"I've seen one like that somewhere," said Father Guthrie, turning it over in his hands. "Phew! Quite a smell to it. Mind if I wash it off?"

"Sure, go ahead," said Andrew. Father Guthrie took the bowl over to the sink, ran the water, and scrubbed at the bowl with a brush. As the weed came off it, the green colour came through — dark green in some places, light green in others.

"I've seen a bowl like this somewhere," said Father Guthrie. "I think it's quite old." He turned it over. On the bottom were the letters FXP. "Hmmmm. Would you leave this with me for a day or so, Andrew?"

"Sure," said Andrew.

That night, just before Andrew went to bed, the telephone rang.

"Andrew?" said Father Guthrie's voice. "I've done a little checking on that bowl. It's French. It goes back two hundred years or more, when all this country belonged to France. And a friend of mine in the museum in Halifax says the museum would probably pay $100 for it, if it's genuine."

"Wow!" said Andrew. "That old bowl?"

"That old bowl. Apparently there are only two others like it, and neither one is in as good condition as this one. Do you want to sell it?"

"Yeah," said Andrew. A bicycle? A wetsuit? It didn't feel right.

"What are you going to do with all that money?"

"Give it to the union," said Andrew.

4

ANDREW was carrying a lunch down to his father, trying to remember to tell Phonse to phone Narcisse LeBlanc in L'Anse au Griffon, when Buck's old van went clattering by, coming away from the picket line. Buck waved at Andrew, and Andrew waved back, wondering how Buck seemed to be in so many different places in the run of a day. He always seemed to have time for everyone. He'd explain something over and over again, patiently, until you understood it. He never seemed to get angry. Andrew had watched him once talking with Billy Morgan and Ambrose Hendsbee. Billy and Ambrose were sour and owly, just spoiling for a fight, but Buck wouldn't fight with them. He just kept on talking, trying one idea after another, until he came up with something that the others could agree with.

"Boy!" said Andrew afterwards. "I'd have been yelling at those two."

Buck just laughed.

"Temper is a luxury," he said. "If you try to force people, they just dig in their heels."

Andrew turned the corner and saw the men down the street, walking back and forth with their picket signs. Just ahead of him was a dark brown car, a sedan, with two men in it. What would two men in a strange car be doing looking at the picket line?

He walked along keeping his eyes on the car. Both men had very short hair, and the one in the passenger seat was holding something up to his face. The driver was just watching the picketers. Andrew walked up beside the car and noticed that the men had shoulder patches. Two round brown hats lay in the back seat. There was a light on the dashboard.

Policemen. Mounties.

Now he could see that the passenger had a camera with a long round barrel poking out of the front of it. A glass lens flashed in the end of the barrel. It was pointed at the picketers.

Mounties taking photographs?

Andrew kept right on walking towards the picket lines, never letting the Mounties know he even saw them, until he met the picketers standing in a group talking seriously.

"I *know* it's a big thing in the province," Phonse was saying. "I know that."

"You see on the news that the students in Halifax think we should keep up the strike?" asked Leo.

"Yeas, and the little newspapers say the same thing," said Phonse. "But the big newspapers and the churches aren't supportin' us at all—"

"Now wait a minute," said Jimmy Parker. "Don't forget Father Guthrie. Some preachers is behind us."

"Well, the odd one here and there," said Phonse. "Look, now, here's Andrew with me lunch."

"Now, the government—" Leo began.

"Dad," Andrew said, "there's two—"

"Hold on a minute, Andrew," said Phonse.

"The government says we should have a union," said Leo. "The labour minister, he said he figured the law was gonna be changed to give us a union."

"But when?" Phonse said. "Someday, fine, but what are we gonna do right now?"

"What about the federal government?" Leo said. "Shouldn't those characters in Ottawa do somethin'?"

"Yeah, they should," Phonse said, looking at his brother.

"They won't do a thing," said Ambrose. "I said right from the start we never should have got into this strike, and now you're seein' why."

"That's right," said Billy Morgan nodding his head.

"Dad—" said Andrew.

"You know, Phonse," said Leo in his mild way, "we could send some of the boys up to Ottawa. Go see the government and tell them they got to do something to get us our union."

"Good publicity, too," said Jimmy Parker cheerfully. "All the Upper Canadian papers and the TV, they'd love to take pictures of us with our rubber boots on under that big clock at Parliament."

"Dad—" said Andrew again. His father started to answer, and then Buck's old van came splashing around the corner and stopped behind the rectory.

"You fellows look all worked up," said Buck.

They told him about the idea of sending a delegation to Ottawa to put pressure on the national government.

"Not a bad idea," said Buck nodding. "We've got a meeting tomorrow night, we should put it to the boys. And we'd have to figure out who to send, too."

"Phonse for sure," said Leo. "I don't know how he can talk into a microphone like he does, but he does it good."

"Ambrose, you'd be a good one to go," said Buck. "How about it?"

"Not me" said Ambrose. "I ain't goin' on TV or in the papers."

"Shy, are you?" chuckled Jimmy.

"Call it anything you like," said Ambrose. "But I ain't goin'."

"Freddy Quinn," said Phonse. "Freddy can hold up that mangled hand in front of the cameras, that'll get the message over."

"Dad," said Andrew, "I got something I want to tell you."

"That's right, you did," said Phonse. "I forgot. What is it?"

"See that brown car up the street?"

"Yeah, what about it?"

"They're Mounties," said Andrew, "and they're taking pictures. What are they doing that for?"

"Say that again, Andy?" said Buck quickly.

"There's two Mounties in that car, taking pictures."

"What in tunket would they want with pictures of us?" asked Jimmy.

"I'd say someone's goin' to court," said Buck thoughtfully. "Me, for one. I'm the bad guy, you know, the troublemaker from outside the province."

"What's the pictures for?" Leo asked.

"To prove there's an illegal strike going on."

"Illegal?" said Ambrose.

"Well, not exactly illegal," said Buck, "but they'll call it illegal. The law doesn't say we can strike, but it doesn't say we can't, either. Anyway, it might be they'll try to charge the leaders with disturbing the peace by provoking an illegal strike, or something like that."

"Well, let 'em try," growled Phonse.

"We can be ready for it," said Buck. "Thanks to Andy, here. Good job you keep your eyes open."

Andrew grinned and didn't know what to say. Then he remembered.

"Oh, and Dad, you're supposed to call Narcisse in L'Anse au Griffon."

"I guess it's about the fish sale," said Phonse. "We got to put the word around today, Jimmy. Everyone that ain't on the picket line tomorrow, go to the bait shed and get ready for a day's fishin'. And then a day peddlin' fish in Halifax."

"Be nice to go fishin'," said Jimmy. "I almost forgot how to do it."

The bait shed was crowded with men and trawl tubs — big open-mouthed wooden buckets. Inside the tubs the men coiled the long lines of trawl — tough cord as thick as a pencil, with pieces of lighter cord tied to it at even spacings. Each of the light cords had a big, wicked-looking hook on the end, and a piece of bait stuck over the tip of the hook.

Scott was helping Andrew cut up some short pieces of light cord. At a workbench along the side of the shed, Phonse and a couple of others were chopping up squid and herring for bait, their huge knives rising and falling with a heavy *thunk! thunk! thunk!* that Andrew could feel shaking the whole benchtop.

"Nice thing, now," said Phonse. "Here I am choppin' bait for you fellers, and I don't even need any for meself."

"You ain't got gillnets out this point in the season, Phonse?" said Freddy Quinn.

"Yeas," said Phonse, "Alfred 'n' Jud put 'em out, and they're catchin' enough for some chowder, anyways."

"I thought everybody was usin' trawl," said Freddy.

"Trawl takes too long to fish," Phonse said. "And we ain't fishin' for to sell it, only to feed people. Feller can run out and haul a few nets in a few hours, no trouble to do that."

"Hey, Andrew," said Scott.

"Sorry," said Andrew looking around. He had been watching the men, forgetting that he was supposed to be cutting off the pieces of light line as Scott measured them. Andrew sawed away at the cord with his knife.

"Holy dyin'," said Paul Nickerson, "you goin' to be a fisherman, young Andrew?"

"Yeah, I guess."

"Time you kept your knife sharp, then," said Paul. "Fisherman with a dull knife is a bad fisherman. Look here."

He took the boys over to the flat, square stone on the workbench. "If them big baitchoppers wasn't sharp, they might bounce off of a fish and hit somethin' else. Like your finger, maybe. Knives got to be sharp. Here, take your knife, and put a little oil on the stone. Keep the blade almost flat, and work the knife round in a circle, see? Get all the blade goin' over the stone. Now bring the blade upright a bit more. Few strokes that way, that's enough. Now run your thumb across the back of the blade. — Not *along* it, Andrew, want to cut yourself? Okay, feel the little ridge at the edge?"

"Yeah," said Andrew. On the side that hadn't touched the stone, a little curl of metal had formed. It felt like a wire along the back of the knife.

"Turn her over, and put her right flat on the stone," said Paul. "Now run her back and forth a couple of times, just to take that ridge off. That's enough. Now touch it to the back of your thumbnail. If it'll take off a shaving, it's sharp. Like this."

He took the knife and stroked the back of his nail with the cutting edge. A paper-thin shaving of thumbnail rolled up in front of the blade.

"*Now* try it," Paul said.

Andrew just touched the knife to a piece of trawl line, and cut it off clean.

"Wow!" said Scott who had been studying the whole process intently.

"That's the way it *should* be," said Paul.

The voices of the men at the workbench had been rising, but now someone cried, "*It's stupid!*" Andrew turned around to see Phonse flying backward across the bait shed and fetching up with a crash against the far wall, his big baitchopper still in his hand. Billy Morgan was shouting at him and coming for him with his own big knife.

Quick as a cat, Freddy Quinn seized Billy's arm and twisted it around behind him. The baitchopper clattered to the concrete floor.

"*You wanna starve?*" Billy yelled. "*You wanna go to jail? Go ahead, you damn fool! But not me, you hear? Not me!*"

"Take it easy, Billy!" said Paul. "Slow down!" He stepped between the two men.

"I'll cut his stupid head off!"

"You and six more, maybe!" Phonse growled. "Come on, I'm ready."

"Lemme go!" snapped Billy. With a jerk he wrenched himself free and strode out the door, slamming it shut behind him.

"You son of a —!" Phonse began, running after him. But Jimmy Parker jumped in front of the door.

"Cool down, Phonse!"

"That slimy little rat!" Phonse snapped. "Said Buck was makin' fools of us. Said all Buck wants is more members to pay dues into the union, give him a raise in pay."

"I don't care," Jimmy said. "You fellers want to go beat each other up, that's fine. We'll go up behind the ball field. But not with them knives in your hands."

"Aaah, forget it," said Phonse. "No good fightin' among ourselves." He took a deep breath. "I just lost me temper, that's all."

"We'll go straighten him out after," said Jimmy. "But let's get this here gear ready first."

Paul picked up Billy's baitchopper from the floor. It had a thick, heavy blade, razor-sharp and gleaming along its cutting edge, and a massive wooden handle. It was as long as Andrew's arm, and heavy as a small axe. Pretty scary weapon, Andrew thought. He'd never expected to see one used that way.

He looked up at Phonse who was cutting bait furiously, the knife thumping hard into the bench. Phonse turned around and looked at Andrew.

"Ah, don't worry about it, Andrew," he shrugged. "Billy and Ambrose, though, them two give me the pip." He sighed. "What I need is some good hard work. I need to go fishin'."

Phonse shook Andrew awake in the middle of the night and they walked down to the wharf in the wet and windy darkness. Alfred already had the motor running in *Dolly C*. Denny and his father Leo were there, too, and Alfred's son Jud who normally fished on the big dragger *Gannet*. Usually only Alfred and Phonse fished in *Dolly C*, but this time the others had come to lend a hand, since the fish would be sold to raise money for the union.

"Gale warnin's, Phonse," said Alfred, as Jud let go the ropes that held the boat to the wharf.

"Not just warnin's," grinned Phonse. "She's blowin' pretty near a gale right now."

It was true. The wind was screeching in the rigging of the little jigger mast in the boat's stern, and its force was making *Dolly C* rock back and forth gently even in the shelter of the wharf.

"Couldn't fish in this weather without all the help," said Alfred.

"Well, there's enough of us," Phonse replied.

As they ran out of the harbour in the dark, the rain splattered all over the boat and streamed down the windshield. A few other boats were going, too — boats that belonged to union men — but instead of twenty or thirty Cape Island boats, Andrew reckoned there couldn't be more than ten, and four of those turned back just outside the harbour.

No wonder. Sometimes Andrew had gone out with his father on days when the sun was bright and the sea was calm or gently heaving. Then a fishing trip was like a vacation with pay, as Alfred liked to say. But today, once they left the shelter of the harbour, the wind hit them like an angry fist, and the boat began the frightening lift and crash! that went on all day. She'd rear up on a huge wave, roll sideways, then come down into the trough with a smack that shook every timber in her and knocked the cups off their hooks down in the little cabin forward. As she hit, the water would explode up and out on each side of the bow. The boat would stagger and then start climbing the next wave, and Andrew would brace himself for the next crash. It felt as though *Dolly C* were coming down on concrete every time. Andrew looked at Denny in the pale light of the instrument panel.

"Some tough boat," Denny grinned.

But if the boat's motion was terrible on the way out, it was even worse once she was idling out on Widow's Bank, the shallow part of the ocean where the men from Widow's Harbour set their nets. With no headway and the engine out of gear, *Dolly C* tossed this way and that, however the waves happened to catch

her. Andrew clutched the side of the doorway and half fell down to the fish pens, holding on for dear life.

"Let's get a bit of sail on her," Phonse said. "Just for to hold her steady while we work. Come on, Andrew."

Andrew followed his father to the stern of the boat, where the short jigger mast stuck up into the sky. He and his father unrolled the rough little sail. The moment they hoisted it up the mast, the boat leaned over a little bit and then held steady.

"That's more like it," said Leo.

The men began hauling the nets, streaming with water, over the side of the boat, disentangling the fish and throwing their wet, silvery bodies into the big wooden boxes on deck where they would stay until they were gutted on the way home. A wave roared up beside them, broke into a smother of white foam, and dropped into the open cockpit, swirling around their feet before it ran out the drains and back into the ocean.

"Bald-headed Moses, Phonse," Alfred grumbled. "What on earth are we doin' out here, fishin' in the devil's own windstorm?"

"Alfred, we ain't fishin'. Nossir, we're raisin' money for the union. It's an absolute, complete different matter."

"Ah!" said Alfred, grabbing the rail for support as the boat gave a wicked lurch. "Is that it? Seems a lot like fishin' to me."

"Tee-totally different," Phonse replied. "No, Alfred,

nobody in his senses goes out fishin' in this kind of weather. Man could get drownded in a gale of wind like this. Nossir, I'm right glad we're working for the union instead of fishin'.'"

"You know somethin'?" Jud said drily. "Seems like bein' on strike is harder work than *workin'*."

Everybody laughed. The men were working with their knees braced hard underneath the side of the boat. At night, when Phonse took his trousers off, Andrew had seen the angry red marks that he'd gotten from working all day pressing his knees up under the rail. Andrew himself was on his hands and knees half the time, picking up fish that had missed the pen and coiling up rope as it came in with the nets. Jud reached for the highflyer, and the boat gave a heavy roll. Jud nearly went overboard, but Phonse grabbed him and held him. Twice they lost big codfish because the boat pitched and brought a wave aboard just as they were untangling the fish from the net. Usually you could see other boats from Widow's Harbour scattered all over Widow's Bank, each one hauling its own nets, but today Andrew could hardly see anyone. The few other boats out there kept falling out of sight between the waves, and he could just catch a glimpse of them now and then, when both the other boat and *Dolly C* were on the crests of waves.

They moved on after each net was emptied, and found another highflyer, one of the tall buoys that marked the position of the nets. They had twelve nets set, and each had to be found, the highflyer brought aboard, and the net reeled in, up from the ocean floor. Everything had to be hauled up in that wild, angry sea, the anchors bashing the planks of the boat, the lines slithering here and there despite Andrew's and Denny's best efforts to coil them and keep them coiled.

Finally it was done, the last net hauled, the last anchor thrown back with a splash into the curling, foaming sea, the last highflyer bobbing astern as *Dolly C* motored away. The men clustered in the wheelhouse again, their breath steaming up the windows while the water from their clothes sizzled on the hot exhaust pipe that ran up through the house.

Alfred swung the wheel, and the boat headed back the way she had come out. Now the wind seemed lighter, and instead of punching into the seas, *Dolly C* wallowed heavily from side to side as the waves rose up behind her, then lifted her stern and set it down as they rolled on past the bow.

"Time to get at it, boys," said Jud, throwing a cigarette overboard. Andrew and Denny went back with Jud and Leo to the fish pens. Leo took out a knife and began picking up one fish after another, slashing the length of their bellies and tossing them to Jud. With one scoop of his hand, Jud removed the fish's innards and threw them overboard. Andrew got out his knife and slit a fish himself, from the vent near the tail up to the throat, between the gills. He tossed the fish to Denny who yanked out the guts and threw the fish in another box. Leo and Jud cleaned four fish in the time it took Andrew and Denny to do one. Andrew tried to set his own rhythm, but it was hard. Some of the fish were half as big as he was. He couldn't throw a fish like that. He had to drag it.

They put the last fish in the box just before *Dolly C* entered the harbour. With blood splashed on their rainsuits, they stood inside the wheelhouse as Alfred steered the boat between the buoys and into the harbour. The wind and sea dropped so fast it seemed almost calm, though the rigging on the mast was still howling.

Dolly C slowly crossed the harbour and tied up at Phonse's wharf in the Tiddle. Two other boats were already there, loading fish into the back of pickup trucks that would carry it to Halifax, Sydney, and other big towns in Nova Scotia, to be sold to people on the street.

By the time Phonse and Andrew walked up to the house for supper, Andrew was stumbling and yawning. They had been gone for thirteen hours.

"Tired?" said Phonse.

"Little bit."

"Been a long day," said Phonse, opening the back door of the house and peeling off his jacket. "Good job of work, though. You know what that catch of fish means?"

"What?"

"Enough money to keep seventy-five families going

for about a week," said Phonse. "Which is a good day's work."

When Andrew opened his eyes the next morning, the sun was streaming in the window. He'd slept late. As he stumbled downstairs, he heard his parents talking.

"How long are you going for?" Laura asked. The kettle began to whistle, and she got up to turn it off and make a pot of strong dark tea.

"Four or five days, I s'pose," said Phonse, his mouth full of porridge. "Takes a long, long day to get up there, Buck said, and I guess we'll stay a couple of days. Maybe stop in Montreal on the way home, see if we can raise some money there."

"Where are you going now?" Andrew yawned.

"Ottawa," said Phonse. "So you better look after things down here for me. Check the boat out morning and evening, for one thing. Keep your ma supplied with fish and berries."

"Yeah, yeah," said Andrew impatiently.

"Don't be owly, now," said Phonse.

"I do that stuff anyways," said Andrew. "Can I use the dory?"

"I guess so," said Phonse. "Since you're looking after things."

"When are you leaving?" Andrew asked.

"Right away," said Phonse. "I got me bag all packed already. Now let's enjoy a cup o' tea before I go, shall we?"

Before Phonse had finished his tea, Buck's van pulled up at the gate. Phonse hugged Laura on the steps.

"Well, good luck," said Laura. "Give 'em a piece of our minds."

"Yeas," grinned Phonse. He kissed her, and hugged Andrew, and they drove away.

That afternoon the fishermen found out why the Mounties had been taking pictures. A tall man in a suit drove down to the picket line, got out of his car with a sheaf of papers in his hand, and started to read them to the men on the picket line. Andrew was playing checkers with Scott on the back porch of the rectory. They stopped the game and ran down to the road.

"Hold on, hold on," said Jimmy Parker. "What in tarnation does that thing mean?"

"It's a court order," said the man in the suit. "It orders you to stop picketing within three days."

"Who's that?" Andrew whispered to Ambrose.

"Roger Firth," said Ambrose softly. "County sheriff."

"We didn't hear nothin' about a court case," Jimmy protested.

"It's an *ex parte* motion," said the sheriff.

"What kind of party?"

"*Ex parte*," said the sheriff again. "It means the judge only heard one side of the case, because it was an emergency. He heard from the company, he didn't hear from the union."

"How does he know the rights and wrongs of it if he only hears one side?" Jimmy demanded.

"Don't ask me," shrugged the sheriff. "All I have to do is read it to you and be sure it's posted where you can see it."

The sheriff reached into his car and got a hammer and a nail, and tacked the papers to the telephone pole.

"Wait a minute," said Jimmy. "We ain't taking this picket line down."

"That's up to yourselves," said the sheriff. "But I'd take it down if I was you."

"Why?"

"Because if you don't, you'll get a big fat fine, and maybe even a jail sentence. Contempt of court is what they call it. You don't do what the court tells you, the court can do what it wants with you. That's all."

"I never heard of anything so rotten in my life," snapped Jimmy.

"I don't think much of it myself, to tell you the truth," said the sheriff. "But I've got a job to do, which is to make sure you know about the order. Now you know about it, that's all I have to do." He got back in his car and drove away.

"I thought people had some rights in this country." raged Jimmy. "Now I find out they can go to law on you, and you don't even know about it."

"Somebody should get in touch with Buck," said Louis Bond.

"How you gonna do that?" Ambrose demanded.

"He's somewhere between here and Ottawa, that's all we know about it."

"Yeah," said Jimmy. "You're right, Ambrose."

"I'm through," said Ambrose. "I ain't goin' to jail, not over any foolish strike."

"Aaaah!" said Louis. "They won't do nothin'.'"

"They won't do nothing to *me*," said Ambrose, "because I won't be here."

"Me neither," said Billy Morgan.

"They're only out to scare us off!" said Jimmy. "You gonna let them do that?"

"I ain't takin' any chances," said Ambrose doggedly. "I'm through." He turned on his heel and started walking away.

"Hey, Ambrose!" said Billy. "I'm comin'."

Jimmy stood with his hands on his hips, watching the two men go.

"They might be serious you know, Jimmy," said Louis uncertainly.

"They might," said Jimmy. "Man, I wish I could talk to Buck. I don't know nothin' about goin' to law."

By supper time the word was all over Widow's Harbour. The phone kept ringing, and Laura kept saying No, she didn't know any more about it, and No, she hadn't heard from Buck and Phonse and the others, and No, she didn't know where they were staying in Ottawa.

"Mom!" called Andrew. "Come look who's on the news!"

"Andrew, I'm on the phone!" Laura scolded.

"Dad's on TV!"

"What!" cried Laura. "Denise, Phonse is on TV, I'll talk to you later. Andrew, move out of the way for heaven's sake—"

The camera had moved slowly across the big lawn in front of the Parliament Buildings while the announcer told the audience about the strike "in tiny Widow's Harbour, Nova Scotia." Then it zoomed in on the group of fishermen on the building's steps, and zoomed closer yet, right in on Phonse's face.

"We seen the minister of labour," said Phonse, "but he wasn't very much help to us."

"What did he say?" asked the reporter.

"Well, he said we didn't have a right to a union," Phonse said wrinkling his nose. "We told him we *got* a union, and that's that, and we ain't gonna stop picketing and striking till we get it recognized."

"What about the injunction?" asked the reporter.

"What's that?" Phonse asked.

"Didn't you hear that a judge in Halifax gave you an order today for the union to stop picketing?"

"I never heard that," Phonse said.

"Well, what do you think of it? Will it make you quit?"

"No," said Phonse. "That judge can take that court order and use it for to wrap fish in. Why can't we have a union? Everybody else has—the plumbers, the welders, the carpenters, even the doctors and lawyers—so why not the fishermen? We ain't gonna stop picketing until we get our union."

"If you don't drop your picket lines, the judge can

send you to jail," said the reporter. "How would you feel about that?"

Phonse grinned over the TV screen.

"Well, I never ever went to jail before," he said, "but I guess there's always a first time. If we got to either call off the strike or go to jail, I guess I'd just as soon go to jail."

Phonse's picture winked off, and the reporter went on to talk about an election somewhere out West, and who was going to win it.

"Dad won't really have to go to jail, will he?" Andrew asked.

"Oh, I don't think so," said Laura, but her voice was shaky. "Now you run off to bed, I got some phone calls to make."

Lying in his bed, Andrew strained to listen. His mother was worried, and fighting mad. She wouldn't show it to him, but she didn't hide it from the other women she phoned.

"I never heard of anything so unfair in my life. They never got a chance to say one word to the judge, and he orders them to give up their union. Well, that's what it means, *give up the union*. Once you take down those picket lines, it's over —"

Andrew tried to imagine what jail would be like. Hard stone walls and a steel gate with bars. After a while he could close his eyes and see a jail cell. But in his mind he couldn't get his father inside it. He tossed under the blankets. Jail, he thought. My father might go to jail, just for walking on a picket line.

5

WHEN Andrew got up in the morning, Laura was walking around the kitchen, humming. Uh-oh, thought Andrew. When his mother hummed, you knew she was planning something.

"Your father called last night, from Ottawa," she said.

"What'd he say?"

"Just that they're on their way home, but they have to stop and talk at the refinery workers' union meeting in Montreal on the way. Ask them for help."

"What about that thing with the judge?"

"The men had a meeting last night," Laura said, "and they decided they're not payin' attention to that, except one or two like Ambrose Hendsbee and Billy Morgan. Ambrose says they're all gonna go to jail. Alfred says if they all go together, it won't be too bad."

The phone rang.

"Andrew?" said Denny's voice. "Mackerel are in at the wharf."

"See you down there," said Andrew.

In front of the fish plant, not far from the wharf, a knot of fishermen were talking excitedly. Andrew stood on the edge of the group and listened. Uncle Alfred looked down at him, and gave him a slow wink.

"I wonder if the fellers at L'Anse au Griffon got these summonses, too," said Jimmy, looking at a paper in his hand.

"Yeas, they did," said Freddy Quinn. "I just called over to Pascal Poirier on the CB radio. Twenty of their members was served this morning."

"When do they got to go to court?" Louis Bond asked. "Friday? Same day as us?"

"They're goin' Thursday, the French fellers from over the bay," said Freddy.

"Well, what we got to do is call this lawyer in Halifax that Buck told me about," said Jimmy. "Better ask him what's goin' on, what we got to do."

"I don't like it," said Paul Nickerson.

"Now you ain't gonna take off like Ambrose and Billy, are you?" demanded Freddy.

"Don't be stupid!" Paul snapped. "But Ambrose got a point. It's one thing goin' on strike. It's another thing goin' to jail. Wonder how much time we'd get."

"Buck thought maybe a week or two."

"That's long enough for the company to get scabs in the plant and get the boats out fishin'."

"Might not be a jail sentence at all, though."

"No, but it might be a month, too. Maybe more, even."

"Anyways, we got to go," said Jimmy. "Meetin' tonight at seven, okay? We can figure it out then."

Muttering and nodding, the men broke up. Some of them walked away in small groups up the street. Half a dozen went back to walking the picket line. Andrew hurried on down to the wharf.

The boys were spaced out all along the government wharf. The mackerel were really running, making ripples on the smooth surface of the harbour as dozens of them rushed after tiny silver minnows, driving the tiny fish into the shallows like frantic slivers of light. Andrew walked out to the end of the wharf where Denny was pulling in mackerel almost as fast as he could get his fishing line into the water. Andrew nodded at Pee Wee, George, Mac, Jeff, Peter, Ernie, Hector. All of them were busy pulling in fish.

With a grin at Denny, Andrew got out his mackerel jigger, the lump of lead shaped like a fish, with a wicked cluster of hooks at the end. He tied it to his line and dropped it over. The mackerel were swirling around the wharf, and one struck his line almost as soon as it hit the water. Up came a mackerel — a sleek, wiggling torpedo with black bars along its side, slapping and flopping on the wharf. With a quick stamp of his boot, Andrew killed it, threw it into his pail, and cast his line over again.

It was a good feeling. Later, Laura would split the mackerel down the back, then lay it out flat in a bucket with salt below and above it. Then the next one, and a layer of salt, and another with another layer of salt, and so on until the bucket was full. They'd snap the lid on it and put it down in the cellar. If you opened the bucket a few days later, you'd find it full of water which the salt had drawn out of the fish. Lying in brine like that, the mackerel would never rot. Months later, Laura could take them out and soak them in fresh water, then boil them for supper.

The mackerel fed like furies for a while, and then suddenly stopped as the warm sunlight began to heat up the water. They would be back in the evening. Andrew and Denny picked up their buckets of fish and started for home. The other boys were laughing and joking together as they headed home, too.

"Look," whispered Denny. "Up on the road there."

Four boys were walking away together. George Jackson, Jeff Ritcey, Peter Thorpe — and Ernie Hendsbee.

Andrew and Denny stood and watched the boys walk away. Ernie turned his head nervously and took a quick look at them.

"Well," said Denny. "Well, well."

As the boys carried their mackerel along the street

by the fish plant, they could only see two men marching with picket signs on their shoulders. Jimmy Parker and Freddy Quinn.

"Where is everybody?" Andrew asked.

"Sick," said Jimmy in disgust. "Or got errands to do. Or didn't get back from the woods yet."

"Any amount of excuses," said Freddy. "Truth is, some of them's scared. Ambrose Hendsbee's been chippin' away at them, tellin' them they can't win, tellin' them they're goin' to jail for sure, tellin' them Skinner'd probably put up wages and stuff if they'd just give up this union nonsense."

"Why ain't that good enough?" Denny asked.

"Because what he gives you today, he can take away tomorrow," said Jimmy. "Once the union's broken up, he can put the wages right down again, and you'd have to start from scratch. But if he breaks a union contract, you can just take him to court, make him live up to the agreement."

"What can you do about the fellows getting scared off?" asked Andrew.

"Just go talk to 'em," said Jimmy. "Which is what we're gonna do as soon as we get some other fellers down here. If you see any of the boys, you tell 'em there's just the two of us here."

"We can go get Scott, anyways," Denny said. "And get Father Guthrie to help, too."

"Good enough," nodded Jimmy. "Off you go, then."

They ran up the rectory steps, full of their worries.

But one look at Scott's face told them that Scott had troubles, too.

"Holy jumpin', what's the matter?" said Denny.

"My father's getting fired," said Scott. "We're going to move again."

"What!" cried Denny and Andrew together.

"You know that Skinner was one of the big members of the church? And Ritcey, and Jackson? Well, they don't come to church any more. They don't give any money. And they got in touch with the bishop and told him to fire my father."

"They can't do that!" said Andrew. "Fire him for what? He's doin a great job, all the fellers say that."

"Fire him for supporting the fishermen," said Scott sadly.

"Oh, man!" said Andrew. Everything was going wrong — the summonses, and now this.

"Ain't there anybody safe from that Skinner?" said Denny.

The back door opened, and Father Guthrie came out. He was smiling, but he looked angry. He took off his glasses and looked down at Andrew and Denny.

"Scott told you what's going on, I guess."

"How can they do that?" Andrew asked. "That's rotten!"

"They may not do it," said Father Guthrie. "They've asked the bishop to transfer me, and he's asked me to go up to Halifax and talk it over with him. He's very concerned that the church people down here aren't happy with my work."

"That church is packed every Sunday!" said Denny.

"With fishermen," said Father Guthrie. "Which is how I think it should be, in a fishing village. But the church has to have money, too, you know. I have to be paid, the building has to be kept up, and I have to run a car. These things cost money, and what a fisherman can give to the church isn't very much compared with what these business people can give."

"Seems like they got you every which way," said Andrew. "The judges and the Mounties and the church—"

"I thought this was supposed to be a free country, Dad," said Scott.

"Well, it's supposed to be," said Father Guthrie. "But you know, if someone has a lot of money and owns a fish plant, and someone else tries to cut into their profit, you can see why they'd fight it any way they could."

"My dad says he thinks the other fish companies are helping Skinner," said Denny.

"I'm sure they are," said Father Guthrie calmly. "You know, there are about forty thousand fishermen in Nova Scotia. Suppose the union gets in here? The union's organizing in other ports, too. If we win here, likely all the companies will fall in line. Pretty soon you're going to have forty thousand fishermen all working together. They could stop the fishing industry cold, striking all together. They could probably throw the government out, if they all voted the same way. There's not too much they couldn't do, in a province the size of Nova Scotia that depends on fishing so much."

"Wow," said Andrew, "they'd run the place."

"Sure they would," said Father Guthrie. "And why shouldn't they? They're the ones who do the work. You don't see Skinner or Ritcey getting their fingers cut off, sitting at their desks. So those men are frightened. They want to stop the union right here. That's why they forced the strike here, and that's why Skinner won't budge. I'm not surprised they went after the bishop to get rid of me."

"But we're going to win!" cried Scott. "We've got to!"

"I don't know," said Andrew. "Some of the men are backing down already. There's only Jimmy and Freddy down there now."

"I'll go down right away," said Father Guthrie, jumping up and looking out the window.

"That's only going to get you in more trouble," said Denny.

"Might as well be hung for a sheep as a lamb," said Father Guthrie. "They need the encouragement. That's what I'm here for."

"We were going to go look for some people for the picket line," said Andrew.

"Good idea," said Father Guthrie. "Put the word around. Maybe Jimmy can come up and help once I'm on the picket line."

"Let's try the garage," said Denny. "Generally a few fellers hanging around there."

As they walked up the street, Scott said, "The old man was wild today."

"Couldn't tell," said Denny.

"You look at his eyes," Scott said. "When you see them really hard and bright, he's mad. They were some bright today."

"Never was a preacher like him in Widow's Harbour before," Denny said. "This rotten strike."

"It's worth it!" said Andrew.

"Is it? If Scott got to move?"

"Yes, it *is*," said Scott fiercely. "But I don't want to move, either."

"Must be something we can do about it," said Andrew, as they turned into the Irving station.

As usual, the inside of the station was dark and cool, like a cave, even on a hot summer day. As usual, three or four men were sitting on milk crates around the cold stove. Louis Bond, Paul Nickerson, Russ Ryan, and Ambrose Hendsbee. They all looked up when the boys came in.

"What's up, young Andrew?" said Russ.

"Jimmy and Freddy is all alone on the picket line," said Denny.

The men all looked at each other, and then looked away. Nobody said anything for what seemed like a long time.

Then Russ stood up.

"We all started into this together," he said quietly. "We should all finish it together, too, whatever it's goin' to be like. I'm goin' down there."

"Me, too," said Paul.

"And me," said Louis, standing up. The three of them looked down at Ambrose.

"You might be right, Ambrose," said Paul. "But I can't live like that."

"Come on," said Russ.

The three of them walked out. Ambrose sat on his milk crate and stared at the boys. Andrew could almost feel the hatred coming out of his eyes. Then Ambrose slowly got to his feet, turned his back on the boys, and walked away up the street.

"Skunk," said Denny, disgusted.

After supper the boys went back to the government wharf for the evening mackerel run. By the time they broke up and went to their separate homes, it was almost sunset.

Andrew took his fish into the back porch and put his gear away. Now where was that mackerel jigger? He looked everywhere and couldn't find it. He poked his head into the kitchen.

"Must have left my jigger on the wharf," he said to Laura. "I'll go down and get it."

"You could leave it till the morning," his mother suggested.

"Naw, someone's likely to grab it."

"Well, go then, but don't be too long. It's almost dark."

Andrew walked down through the town in the

twilight. The western sky was still a blaze of orange and yellow, and the bottoms of a few dark, scattered clouds seemed to be on fire.

"Hello, there, Andrew," said a bulky shadow in front of the fish plant.

"Hello, Louis," said Andrew.

"You're out late."

"Left some stuff on the wharf," said Andrew. He went on quickly, anxious to find the jigger while he still had enough light to see it. He trotted along beside the tall wire fence around the parking lot, then went on by the high wall of the fishmeal plant, and turned left onto the wharf. The fishmeal plant was built right beside the wharf, walling it off for half its length.

He hurried on down to the end of the wharf and began to search for his jigger, walking back and forth across the heavy planks, pale green with their anti-rot stain. Perhaps the jigger had been kicked down between the planks and was lying wedged there. Or possibly it had been kicked right off the wharf. Maybe someone had just picked it up and taken it home. If anyone turned up with it he'd know it, because he had cut a deep groove in one of its sides.

The sun was just setting in the Tiddle, falling through the narrow channel between the rocky shores like a flaming coal from a beach fire sliding down the sky. Andrew watched it for a moment. When it touched the water he almost expected to hear it hiss. Once it touched the horizon it seemed to fall down behind it terribly fast.

Standing silently on the edge of the wharf, Andrew suddenly heard voices. He looked around, startled. He hadn't noticed anyone else on the wharf. Somewhere close by, two men were speaking very quietly. He couldn't make out what they were saying.

In the gathering darkness, a door swung open from the fishmeal plant. Two men walked onto the wharf. Andrew still couldn't make out what was being said, but one of the men was Skinner, the manager.

The other man was taller and spoke more softly, but with a sort of whine in his voice. Andrew squatted down, wanting to see without being seen. He recognized that voice. Who was it, and why would he be talking with Skinner so secretively?

Suddenly he knew who it was. It was Ambrose Hendsbee.

6

ANDREW hurried home thinking about Ambrose and Skinner. As he approached the house, he saw Buck's van and Jimmy's car.

Phonse was home!

Andrew broke into a run. Before he reached the back door, he could hear the talk and laughter. Inside the kitchen, a whole gang of fishermen were drinking beer, drinking tea, and talking furiously. In the middle was a knot of men around Phonse and Buck. Andrew weaseled in among their legs and ran to hug his father.

"Well, young feller!" Phonse said, pulling Andrew to him with a huge hand on his shoulder. "Make out all right without me?"

"Did our best," Andrew grinned.

"Good thing," said Phonse. "You better get ready to do it for another month."

"What?"

"Looks like your old man's going to be staying in the government hotel," said Phonse. "The fellers from L'Anse au Griffon got three weeks in jail, and the officers of the local got a month. Either that or drop the picket lines and apologize to the court, and they wouldn't do it."

"A month in jail!" cried Andrew.

"They thought it might be day or two," said Russ. "Guess they were surprised."

"Did we get a lot of press coverage in Nova Scotia?" Buck asked.

"Well, I guess!" said Laura. "It was on the front page in Halifax every day for a week, and there's reporters coming down from one of the big magazines in Toronto, and a TV crew from Sydney. But you have to turn right around and go to Halifax for that racket over the injunction, don't you?"

"Yeas," said Phonse. "But we thought we'd have one night at home, anyways."

"You hear about Father Guthrie, Buck?" asked Jimmy.

"No, what?" Buck said.

"Tryin' to fire him, because he's for the fishermen," said Jimmy. "The big shots don't go to his church since the strike, and it's costin' money. So that's it, he's got to go."

"Well, it ain't quite like that," said Laura. "But the bishop says he's concerned about it, and he wants to see Father Guthrie."

"Seems like everythin's goin' wrong," said Freddy looking gloomy. "Everybody's against us — the Mounties, the courts, the newspapers, and now they're gettin' at a man like that."

The room fell quiet. Nobody said anything.

"Aaah!" said Phonse suddenly. "We can beat 'em all. We got the people with us, everywhere we went on this trip. We picked up $2,000 from the unions in Montreal, too. It ain't all bad news."

"That's right," said Jimmy. "The harder they hit us, the more we hit back." He took a quick poke at Freddy, who came back with a hard smack on Jimmy's cheek with his good hand. Everyone laughed.

"Come on, boys," said Jimmy. "Court in the morning. Bus leaves at 5:30, got to be in Halifax by 10:00. And Phonse needs some sleep."

Reluctantly, the fishermen moved out. Buck said he'd sleep in the van, right outside the house. Jimmy hustled the last stragglers out and closed the door behind him. Andrew looked at his parents, and at Buck. All the others were gone.

"Jimmy's right," said Phonse yawning. "All the sleep I had lately was in the back of that old van, bouncin' along the highways."

"Wish I was goin' up there with you to Halifax," said Laura looking sadly at Phonse. "Don't seem right, you goin' all by yourself."

"Well, all the boys are together, and we're all in the same spot," said Phonse. "I'd like to have you, but I ain't alone. And you're needed down here to handle the money and take care of Andrew." He turned to Andrew. "Now you're goin' to be in charge again. You check that boat every day while I was gone?"

"Yep," said Andrew. "Mooring lines were chafing one time, so we wrapped 'em with rags."

"Good for you. Start the engine at all?"

"No."

"Better do that from now on. Start her up and run her for fifteen or twenty minutes every three or four days. Keep her limber and keep the battery charged up. You check the oil on her?"

"Didn't need to. I didn't run her."

"Before you start her, check the water and oil. And check the oil in the gearbox, too."

"All right," said Andrew.

"Who's going to keep up the picket line?" Laura asked.

"There's a few of the fellers that weren't named to go to Halifax," said Phonse. "Ambrose and Billy, for two. And Paul Nickerson, and John Cavanaugh."

"Dad," said Andrew, "I got something to tell you about Ambrose."

"What's that?"

"Jimmy says he's been pickin' at the men, tryin' to get them to call the strike off."

"Well, he never was a big supporter," said Buck.

"Yeah, but today I went in the garage and he was tryin' to talk Louis and Paul and Russ out of goin' on the picket line. And then just now when I went for my jigger, the side door at the plant opened — you know, the door right on the wharf — and out comes Skinner talking to Ambrose, and both of them looking around to be sure nobody saw them.

"Well, that *skunk!*" said Phonse savagely.

"Tell me about it, Andy," said Buck.

"Not much to tell. I couldn't really hear them, just saw them. But it seemed like they were makin' plans or something."

"I didn't think Ambrose would do that," said Buck sadly.

"Do what?" Laura demanded.

"Well, it sounds like he's working for the company now," Buck said. "He helps Skinner break the strike, and then there's a good job for Ambrose once that plant starts working again. Maybe he'll go skipper on one of the draggers or something like that."

"I'll clean him!" said Phonse, thumping his fist on the table. "I'll murder that son of a —"

"What can he do now?" Buck said quietly. "It's too late for the other boys to quit. We've got to go to court, and they're into it just as much as you and me. We'll deal with it when we're finished with the courts." He turned to Andrew. "That's twice you helped us by keeping your eyes open. You're a regular Sherlock Holmes."

Andrew grinned.

"One thing you can do is just keep an eye on him, you and the other boys," Buck said. "Maybe you'll see something hanging around with Ernie."

"None of us seen Ernie for days and days," said Andrew. "He's hanging around with Jeff Ritcey and George Jackson."

"Ah," said Buck. "Well, you know who to watch out for. Just watch out for them, that's all."

Phonse's idea of an early night wasn't so very early after all, Andrew decided as he drifted off to sleep, hearing his parents still talking at the kitchen table. In the morning he heard their voices, opened one sleepy eye, and saw that the sun was not up yet. He would just lie in bed a little longer, and then get up to say good-bye to his father.

"Take care of things, son," Phonse was saying in his ear. Andrew sat up in bed. His father was freshly shaven and wearing the suit he usually wore to weddings and funerals.

"I was gettin' up—" Andrew began.

"Naw, you need your sleep," said Phonse grinning. Then his face turned serious. "You're gonna have a big load to carry while I'm gone, you know."

"I can do it."

"Sure you can. You're a good man." Phonse fell silent a moment, just looking at Andrew. "I'm proud of you," he said at last. "I'm glad I'm your old man." He turned very quickly and walked out.

"Dad!" shouted Andrew.

"Yeah?" Phonse poked his head back in the door.

"I'm glad, too."

Phonse made a face at him and hurried down the stairs. Andrew got out of bed and stood on the cold linoleum, watching Phonse stride out of the yard and down the road to meet the bus. I wonder when I'll see him again, Andrew thought. I wonder what it's like going to jail?

Andrew heard the story of the courtroom in Halifax afterwards, from Phonse and Jimmy and the others. He heard it so often and so completely that it seemed as though he had been there. The courtroom had high ceilings, very fancy woodwork, and a picture of the Queen up behind the judge. The judge started out about what the charge was and how serious things had become in Widow's Harbour, and Phonse studied the ceiling, not paying very much attention.

The judge said that when the courts decided a thing, then it had to be done, and if people wouldn't do it, they had to be forced. Otherwise, what was the point of having a court at all, if the court couldn't make a decision and know it would be followed?

"Now," said the judge, "when someone refuses to obey the court, we say he is showing contempt for the court, and that's what you're charged with, contempt of court. This court made an order to you men to stop picketing, and you didn't stop."

He stared down at the two rows of fishermen in the front of the courtroom, lined up like so many boys in front of a teacher. The judge was a serious-looking gray-haired man in a black gown, sitting way higher than anyone else in the room, and in front of him there was a woman tapping away on what looked like a little silent typewriter, taking notes.

"All you have to do," said the judge after a moment, "is to apologize to the court for disobeying that order, and agree to obey it from now on. If you do that, I can simply send you all home to your families. But if you continue to show contempt for the court, then I'll have no choice but to punish you very severely. Do you all understand what I've said?"

Nobody said anything at all.

"Very well," said the judge. "Then the first man I want to have brought before me is — let's see." He looked down at his desk and rummaged through some papers. Then he looked down at another man in a dark suit.

"Swear in Alphonse Belmont Gurney," said the judge.

"Alphonse Belmont Gurney," said the man in the suit. Phonse got up and walked slowly to a chair that the man pointed at. He put his hand on a Bible and promised to "tell the truth, the whole truth, and nothing but the truth, so help me God."

"Now, Mr. Gurney," said the judge. "You were in Ottawa last week."

"That's right," said Phonse.

"What were you doing there?"

"We went for to see the minister of labour," said Phonse, "and to try to get our story across to the whole country."

"After your visit to the minister, were you interviewed on a television newscast?"

"Right," said Phonse.

"Did you say this: *that judge can take that court order and use it for to wrap fish in? We ain't gonna stop picketing until we get our union?*"

"Well, I don't remember exactly what I said," Phonse replied. "Maybe it was something like that."

"Not 'something like that,' Mr. Gurney. I believe those were the exact words."

"Well, I wasn't takin' notes," Phonse replied. "I don't recall exactly, but it was along them lines."

"I *was* taking notes," said the judge. "I was watching that newscast. I could hardly believe my ears."

"Well," Phonse shrugged, "if you was takin' notes, you prob'ly got it right."

"Very well," said the judge. "Now, did you understand what I said about the seriousness of the charge against you?"

"I understood it," said Phonse, "but that don't mean I necessarily agreed with it all."

"Explain what you mean."

"Well, you said everybody got to agree to obey the law," said Phonse, sticking out his chin a little. "That's good enough, most times. But whatever judge made that court order, he didn't ask about our side of the thing. He only listened to the comp'ny."

"I made that order myself," said the judge.

"Well, why didn't you give us a chance to speak onto

it?" said Phonse. "How can you know the rights and wrongs if you don't hear both sides?"

"It's an emergency procedure," said the judge. "There wasn't time to hear both sides."

"Why wasn't there?" Phonse asked. "The strike's been going on since three months, and you give us three days to take down the pickets. I don't see what the rush was all about."

"I suppose you're entitled to your opinion," said the judge.

"Yeas, and it's only my opinion," said Phonse. "But what other opinion have I got to go on? The law says fishermen ain't got a right to have a union. The company can cheat them, cut their pay, fire them, make them work on boats that ain't safe, and the fishermen can't do nothin' about it. Anybody else can have a union, but not the fishermen. Well, that may be law, but it ain't right."

"So you intend to continue picketing?"

"I got nothin' against the court, sir," said Phonse. "But if we quit picketin', that's the end of the strike, and the end of the strike is the end of the union. And I ain't workin' on them boats any more without a union."

"Thank you," said the judge briskly. "I think you've made your position perfectly clear." He turned to the lawyer for the fishermen, who was sitting beside Buck. "Mr. Melcher, I'm going to call a half-hour recess. I suggest you use the time to try to talk some sense into your clients."

"All rise," called the clerk. Everyone stood up, and the judge walked out. The fishermen and their friends moved out to the lobby, smoking and talking excitedly.

"You told him good, Phonse," said Jimmy.

"That was just right, boy," said Russ. A young man with long hair and faded jeans came over to Phonse and shook his hand. He was wearing a T-shirt that said *DALHOUSIE UNIVERSITY.*

"Congratulations, sir," said the student. "That was really fine."

Phonse nodded, and the lawyer took him by the arm and steered him into a room beside the lobby. The other fishermen followed behind. Jimmy Parker stood at the door, keeping everyone else out.

"Well," said the lawyer after the door was closed, "he's very determined. I'd say you either apologize and take down your picket lines, or else you're going to jail for two months or more. It's up to you."

"What do you think, Buck?" asked Russ Ryan.

"I don't know," said Buck slowly. "The reason he's so sticky is the fellows from L'Anse au Griffon. He sent them to jail for a month, and they laughed at him. But Phonse summed it up pretty well in there. If you apologize, they've broken the union. They'll know they can make us back down every time, and we'll never get anywhere with the company. On the other hand, I can't really advise you to go to jail. You've fought a good fight, but if you wanted to quit I wouldn't blame you."

108

"It ain't fair!" growled Russ.

"No," said Buck sadly, "it ain't fair, Russ. But it's legal."

The men were silent for a moment, looking at one another, trying to figure out what the others wanted to do. Then Phonse stood up.

"I don't know about the rest of you fellers," he said, "but me, I'd rather go to jail. Two months or two years, it don't matter. I done what I figured was the right thing, and I ain't makin' no apologies to anybody, and that's it."

The others nodded, and then Russ spoke up.

"I'm with Phonse," he said. "We gone this far. No point quittin' now."

Again the nods and the murmurs of agreement. Buck looked at the fishermen, and his face was very serious.

"Anyone think the other way?" he said. "Don't go kidding yourselves. You go along with Phonse, and you'll have your supper in a jail cell tonight."

Louis Bond stood up.

"Look here," he said, "when I was comin' down here on the bus, I figured we better apologize and forget about it. And maybe that *is* the best thing to do, but when I get right down to brass tacks I can't do it. Go in there and say I'm sorry? Phonse here, he's right. I done nothin' to be sorry for, and I *ain't* sorry, and I don't feel good about lyin' and sayin' I *am* sorry."

They went back into the courtroom. The judge entered and called Phonse to the witness stand again.

"You've had a chance to think things over," said the judge. "Will you apologize to the court and agree to obey the injunction?"

Phonse shook his head.

"No, sir," he said. "I ain't troubled by what I done. I think it was right."

The judge turned to the lawyer.

"Mr. Melcher, is that the opinion of all your clients?"

"Yes, Your Honour, it is."

"Is Mr. Poulos here in court?"

"Here, Your Honour," said Buck standing up.

"Mr. Poulos," said the judge, "did you instruct these men not to apologize?"

"No, Your Honour."

"Will you instruct them to obey the injunction?"

"I can't do that, Your Honour," said Buck. "I can *ask* them, but I can't *tell* them."

"What do you mean by that?"

"Just what I say, Your Honour. The members of the union elect me to do what *they* want, not the other way around. I *will* ask the men to consider what they're doing, but I can't order them." Buck turned to the fishermen gathered around him. "You've all heard what His Honour has said," he told them. "Is there anyone here that wants to ask for another recess to talk about it some more, or that wants to apologize right now? Remember that you might be facing a long jail sentence. Nobody would blame you if you did what he asks."

Phonse looked at Buck. If Buck told them to apologize, he thought, they'd probably do it. Not because he was their boss, but because he was Buck, and they trusted him. But nobody said anything.

"You're sure about this?" Buck asked the men.

Russ Ryan turned to Buck. Anyone could see he was boiling.

"You tell that judge," Russ growled, "that Phonse said it right. We done the right thing, and we ain't sorry, and we ain't gonna lie about it just to stay out of jail."

"Very well," the judge sighed. "The decision of the court is this. Mr. Poulos and the others, except Alphonse Gurney, are to be remanded in custody for a week." He gazed down at the fishermen. "What I'm doing is ordering that you be held in jail for a week. I'm not sentencing you, but you'll come back here after that week in jail, and then I'll sentence you. The sentence will depend on whether or not the picket lines are removed by that time."

He turned to Phonse.

"Mr. Gurney. I gave one-month sentences here yesterday, and I saw smiles and laughs on the faces of the men who received them. Very well. The picketing must be stopped. I'm afraid I have no choice but to give you a sentence that will convince you and the others to stop it."

He paused, and the courtroom fell so quiet you could hear people breathing.

"I sentence you," said the judge, "to eight months in jail. Court is adjourned."

Everyone gasped. Phonse stared at the judge. Eight months! He felt as though he had been hit between the eyes with a hammer.

7

"*EIGHT months!*" cried Laura. "*Eight months!* Oh, Andrew!"

"He won't be home for hunting season," said Andrew, trying to take it in. "He won't be home for Christmas, even. He won't be home till next spring."

"How can they put a man in jail for eight months for standing up for his rights?" asked Denise Ryan, who had just come running over with the news from Halifax. "They don't hardly jail them that long for murder!"

"That judge figures that's gonna break the strike," said Laura. "He figures that's gonna get rid of the picket line."

"He might be right," said Denise.

"No!" cried Laura. "If we let them get away with this — no, Denise, we can't!"

"What are we gonna do about it?" asked Denise.

"What if *we* do go down on that picket line?" asked

Laura. "I mean it, what if all the women and children go down on that picket line? Are they going to send you and me and Andrew to jail? Those men worked so hard to win this strike, we just *can't* let them lose now."

A gust of rain swept against the windows, like a rush of tiny feet. Outside, Andrew could see the tops of the trees swaying. Even the weather seemed to be angry.

"You know, we could do that," said Denise thoughtfully. "No court order says we can't, does it?"

"No, it doesn't," said Laura. She laughed bitterly. "If you'd said to me at the beginning of this thing that I'd end up on the picket line myself, I'd have told you you'd gone foolish. But if we don't go, they lose, isn't that right?"

"That's about the size of it," said Denise. "You're right, Laura, we should do that. And we should get *all* the women into it, too."

"Well, we'll break up the list of members between us," said Laura. "You phone half and I'll phone half. And however many I get, we'll be down on that picket line in an hour."

"I can go down now, Mom," said Andrew. "I can get Denny and Scott and Pee Wee and maybe some of the other guys —"

"Good idea," said Laura. "Off you go."

Andrew got up and started for the door.

"Andrew!" called Laura. "Can't you see that rain? Put your slicker on!"

Andrew sighed, put his slicker on, and hurried down to Scott's house. Paul Nickerson and John Cavanaugh were the whole picket line, and they were sitting around the stove in the rectory basement, looking unhappily out at the rain.

"It's only a shower," said Andrew poking his head in the basement. "Mom and Denise and some others are comin' down to go on the picket line. I'm going on it, too."

"The *women* are going on the picket line?" said John with his eyes wide.

"Yep," said Andrew. "See you in a minute."

Ten minutes later, when the rain had stopped, the two fishermen and the three boys were walking back and forth in front of the fish plant with the signs on their shoulders.

"How d'you feel about Phonse gettin' eight months?" asked John.

"Not too good," said Andrew. "But he didn't give up."

"That's right," said Paul. "He's no quitter, Phonse. But I wonder what he feels like right now."

"Feel a lot better if he knew the picket line was still up," said John. "Hello, Myrtle!"

"Got another sign, boys?" asked Myrtle Parker. "Denise and Laura and them's comin' down pretty soon."

"Here," said Andrew. He gave her his sign — *ON STRIKE FOR ALLIED FISHERMEN'S UNION* — and started for the rectory to fetch another sign.

"Hey, Andrew!" shouted Paul. "Run up to the store while you're at it, and grab me an orange pop, will you? Here!"

Andrew whirled around, took Paul's money, bent his head into the wind, and ran up beside the rectory to the main street. He ducked into Ritcey's General Store, pulled a bottle of pop from the cooler and went over to the counter with the money. Frank Ritcey was standing behind the cash register, talking with the Baptist minister. The minister glared at Andrew and then looked away without speaking.

"Well, now, Andrew," said Ritcey, taking the money. "You see how all this foolishness about the union has landed your father in jail, for eight months."

"They should all go to jail," said the minister.

"They all will, I imagine," said Ritcey. "It's a pretty drastic way to end the strike, but they're a stubborn lot."

"It ain't endin' the strike," said Andrew.

"They won't be able to picket when they're all in jail," said Ritcey.

"I ain't in jail," said Andrew. "My mom's not in jail. There's lots of us to go on that picket line yet."

"Good heavens," said the minister. "Innocent children working for that villain Poulos!"

"He ain't a villain!" cried Andrew. "He's the best damn thing that ever happened in this town!"

Quick as a flash, Frank Ritcey reached over the counter and cuffed Andrew hard enough to make his head ring.

"You watch your language in this store!" he snapped. "And especially when there's a man of God here."

"Man of God!" yelled Andrew. "That thing!" He grabbed Paul's pop and ran out of the store. He was boiling mad, and he kept wanting to go back and jam the pop bottle right into Ritcey's face. No wonder Jeff Ritcey is such a skunk, he thought. He was so busy thinking of things he would have said that he walked straight into Ambrose Hendsbee and spilled pop on him.

"Watch where you're goin!" snapped Ambrose. "What do you think you got eyes for?"

"Sorry," said Andrew stepping around him.

"Where are you goin' in such a rush?"

"Picket line," said Andrew. He looked Ambrose straight in the eye. "We ain't *all* chicken, you know."

With a snarl of rage, Ambrose grabbed for him, but Andrew had danced away. "Cock-a-doodle-doo!" crowed Andrew. "Cock-a-doodle-doo!" Ambrose lunged for him again, and again Andrew danced away, crowing like a rooster. Ambrose ran heavily after him, and Andrew kept running and laughing. Suddenly Ambrose stopped. Andrew looked around. His mother was coming down the street with Denise.

"What's all this?" snapped Laura. "Ambrose Hendsbee, what do you think you're doing with that boy?"

"Goin' to give him what he deserves!" Ambrose snorted. "Nobody talks saucy to me and gets away with it."

"Saucy?"

"He called me a chicken. He made chicken noises at me."

Andrew looked at his mother. Behind her serious face he could feel her laughter trying to break through.

"Did he, now?" asked Laura. "Called you a chicken, did he?"

"That's right," scowled Ambrose. "Course, the kind of father he's got, and all —"

"Well, you know," said Laura gravely, "he ain't actually the only one in this town who thinks you belong in a hen house."

Ambrose spluttered, and got red in the face, and looked as though he were going to burst. Denise whooped with laughter.

"Some high and mighty for a woman with a jail-bird husband, ain't you?" Ambrose finally exploded.

"Better a jailbird than a chicken," Laura snapped. "Come on, Andrew, you'll be getting feathers all over you. I don't know why you hang around with the likes of this one."

For a moment Andrew was afraid Ambrose was actually going to hit his mother, he was so mad. But

Laura didn't give him the chance. She took Andrew by the elbow and steered him firmly back to the picket line. When they turned the corner onto the waterfront, she finally burst out laughing, and that got Denise going again. Paul, John, Myrtle, and the others all wanted to know what had happened, and when Laura told them, they broke out in laughter as well.

But they turned angry when Andrew told them about Ritcey and the minister.

"If that was my son," said Paul, "I'd go knock that Ritcey character right over the head with that cash register."

"All he thinks about is that cash register anyways."

"Someone else's kid, who does he think he is?"

"Who's this, now?"

They all turned to look at the old red car that was coming around the corner, full of men in coveralls and work clothes. It pulled up beside them, and six men got out. The driver came up to Paul.

"You the fishermen that's on strike?"

"Couple of us are, yeah," said Paul warily.

The driver put out his hand.

"Shake, brother. We were all workin' on a new building down to Monkstown when we heard about that feller gettin' eight months. Well, I said to the boys, that's it. No way we're gonna go on workin' when a man's been sent to jail for eight months just because he wants a union. We're union men, our place is down on that picket line ourselves."

"Got some more signs?" asked a burly, dark-haired man in coveralls.

"Sure we do!" said Paul. "Sure we do! Boys, I can't tell you how much this means to us. We were gettin' pretty down in the mouth, I can tell you."

"They can't get away with it," said the dark-haired man. "Not if all the union people stick together."

"You know," said Paul, "with you fellers here, this picket line is just as big as it ever was. Ain't that somethin', with most of the boys in jail?"

An hour later a van full of papermakers from the mill at Port Esperance pulled up on the picket line. They had walked off their jobs, too, and come down to support the fishermen. The picket line was beginning to look bigger than ever.

Late in the afternoon the rain started again, and the wind rose. Fog began drifting in, and the day turned black and miserable.

"Those guys in the plant can't even see we're out here," smiled one young papermaker. "We might as well go home, boys, and come back again in the morning."

They left, and a little later the construction workers left, too. Father Guthrie came out and invited the fishermen and their families to come into the rectory and see the supper-time news on television. He was sure it would have something about the strike.

The TV news started out with a report on the

strike, and showed pictures of a rally in support of the fishermen right in front of the courthouse in downtown Halifax. Then the reporter came back on the screen to say that workers had walked off the job in sympathy at different plants all over Nova Scotia — in the coal mines, at the steel mill, at the paper mill, at construction projects.

"Meanwhile, the government has admitted the fishermen's cause is just, but Labour Minister Garfield today refused to commit the government to any immediate action," said the reporter. The picture changed to a short man in a suit. A sign on the screen said *CLARENCE GARFIELD — NOVA SCOTIA MINISTER OF LABOUR.*

"The government agrees that fishermen should be allowed to have unions," said the minister, "and I can understand that people are upset at seeing family men jailed because of the strike in L'Anse au Griffon and Widow's Harbour. But the fact remains that the present law does not allow fishermen to form unions. We expect to change that law as soon as the Legislature is called into session, but in the meantime the existing law has to be obeyed."

"Does that mean you won't do anything about Alphonse Gurney's sentence?" asked the reporter's voice.

"No, no," said the minister quickly. "The people in my department are looking at ways to get all the fishermen out of jail. But if the fishermen themselves won't compromise, you know, it's pretty difficult. I don't see how you can expect the courts to back down."

People groaned and muttered in the rectory basement. Father Guthrie shook his head.

"They're just trying to weasel out of doing anything. All the same, they must be pretty worried by all the sympathy strikes around the province."

"What about your own job, Father?" asked Denise. "Any news?"

"I'm going up to Halifax to see the bishop tomorrow," said Father Guthrie.

"Does that bishop know we don't want you moved?" John asked. "I only went to church since you're here, and if he pulls you out you'll never see me in that place again."

"Wait a minute," Father Guthrie objected. "Even if the bishop makes a mistake, that doesn't mean you should throw out the whole church."

"If the church can't support the people in it," said John, "then I got no time for the church."

"We should make a petition to that bishop," said Denise excitedly. "Write him a letter and everybody sign it."

"Right!" said Laura. "I'll write it up right now." And the next thing they knew, it was done. Everyone signed it, and John said he'd take it around the village the next morning.

"If you don't want to give it to the bishop, don't give it to him," said Laura. "But you'll have it, if you need it."

Outside, the rain and fog continued. The picketers stayed in the rectory basement most of the evening, venturing out now and then to take a turn past the fish plant, "just to be sure they know we ain't gone away," as John Cavanaugh put it. Denise wondered if there was any real reason to keep the picket line up all day and all night. Yes, said John. If they didn't, the company could move truckloads of frozen fish out of the plant to market, or it could bring in dozens of scabs in the middle of the night and have the trawlers out at sea and fishing before anyone got down to the plant in the morning.

"When we're here, they don't know what we might do to stop them," John said. "So they don't take a chance. But just let them think they can get away with something, and they'll try it."

"I guess we better set up shifts for night duty," said Denise. "No point all of us stayin' down here all night long."

"I don't mind staying," said Laura.

"Yes, but you got Andrew to think about," said Denny's mother, Marge. "And I got Denny."

"All right," said Laura, "I tell you what. I'll take the boys down to my place and put them to bed. You stay here till two or three in the morning, and then come get me, and I'll finish the night out."

"I'd like to stay, Mom," said Andrew.

"Are you joking?" demanded Laura. "You're going home to bed, young man, and that's *it*."

"Aw, Mom!"

"Don't *Aw, Mom* me," said Laura. "We might as well go right now."

They struggled into their rain clothes and struck out into the night. The street lights were swaying in the breeze, and there were tiny ripples on the puddles in the road. The wind behind them plastered their clothes against their bodies, and made it hard to speak. They could only see a few paces in front of them because of the drizzle and fog.

They found the gate to the yard and ran for the house. Dripping and glistening, they stood in the back porch, peeling off their rainwear. Suddenly Andrew felt his father's absence. Phonse was gone, and he was going to be gone for a long time. It was almost as though he were dead, and—

"*Dolly C!*" he shouted, struggling back into his jacket. "Denny, come on! I didn't even look at her today!"

"Blowin' a gale, too," said Denny.

Laura looked at them, started to say something, and then thought better of it. She knew even better than the boys that *Dolly C* was the family's living. And in weather like this, banging against the wharf, she could be badly damaged in no time at all. She handed Andrew a flashlight.

"Be careful!" she said. "It's slippery out there."

"We will!" Andrew's words were flung over his shoulder as the boys rocketed out the door and slammed it behind them.

They raced down the dark path, slipping and sliding on the patches of bare rock and soaking grass. Andrew's flashlight made a faint hole in the blackness. Then they were on the wharf, pounding past the gear shed along the narrow walkway.

They stopped, sharply, at the end of the wharf. Andrew swung his flashlight along the black water. *Dolly C* was gone!

No, there she was. Not gone, but going. She was drifting slowly away from the end of the wharf, pushed by the wind. I can't reach out to grab her, Andrew thought, but we could jump aboard —

He stumbled, his foot slipping on something flat on the planks. He caught his balance again and called to Denny.

"Jump!"

Without looking behind him, Andrew ran a couple of steps and leaped over the end of the wharf. He felt himself flying over the narrow space of water between the wharf and the boat. Then he was skidding along the slippery deck in the wide cockpit, catching at the fish boxes until he fetched up against the side deck.

He heard a thump behind him and a small splash in the water. Denny came slithering over the deck until he hit the side deck next to Andrew.

"Oooof!"

"What was that splash?" Andrew asked. He was already ducking into the cabin, looking for the spare key to start the motor.

"Kicked something overboard when I jumped. Something on the wharf."

"Huh," said Andrew barely hearing him. On a night as dark as this, thick with fog and rain, the boat could be right beside the wharf and they wouldn't see it. He had to start the engine, fast. He had to get *Dolly C* back to the wharf.

He found the key on its nail behind the stovepipe, scrambled back into the wheelhouse and slid the key into the switch. When he turned it, the big truck engine started at once, with a barking roar that faded into a soft steady muttering as Andrew cut it back to an idle. He checked all the gauges on the instrument panel. Everything was running fine. He switched on the clear-view, the spinning circle of glass that kept itself clear long after a windshield wiper would have quit. Denny reached up and clicked on the spotlight on the wheelhouse roof. The beam cut a swath through the night, revealing nothing but blowing rain and dark, choppy water.

"Where's that wharf, now?" Denny asked.

"Back behind us, I guess," said Andrew. He slid the gear lever forward, and the engine slowed down as the propeller bit the water and thrust the boat forward. He swung the wheel all the way over to the left, and *Dolly C* turned in a wide, slow curve.

"You should get the dock lines ready, Denny."

Denny moved carefully up the narrow side deck beside the wheelhouse, and then up to the heavy samson post in the centre of the foredeck. Andrew stared into the darkness over the bow, wishing he could claw aside the curtain of rain and catch sight of the little jetty. Then Denny swung in through the open door and dropped to the wheelhouse floor beside him.

"Andrew," said Denny seriously, "look at this."

He was holding out a short piece of rope. Its end was as neat and clean as the end of a big sausage. Andrew stared at it.

"That line's been cut," said Denny.

"Yeah," said Andrew slowly. His mind was racing. "Must just have been cut when we got there. The boat was right by the wharf still."

Denny ducked out of the wheelhouse for a moment and then came back. "Stern line's cut, too," he reported.

"Holy whistlin'," said Andrew. "Where's that jetty, anyway? We should be seein' it by now."

"Goin' pretty slow," said Denny.

"I ain't gonna crack her head-on into that wharf," Andrew replied. "Or on the rocks, either."

"No rocks right by the wharf," Denny pointed out.

"Yeah, but are we by the wharf?" asked Andrew. "We don't know."

"Night like this, it wouldn't be hard to go right past it."

"We'll just have to chug along till we see something," Andrew said. "Then we'll know where we are."

The two boys stood right up against the wind-shield, peering into the rain. Andrew glanced down.

"Aw, *no!*"

"What?"

"I never even thought to look at the compass," said Andrew, trying to figure it out as he spoke. "The wind was in the east, right? But look at that compass. We're heading west now, right exactly away from the jetty. She must have got turned around before we got the motor goin'."

"Turn her around again," said Denny.

"Yeah. Let's try that." Andrew swung the wheel again, bringing the compass around until the pointer on it lay over the big *E*. Not a sign of the shore, not a boat or a rock or anything. They must be out of the Tiddle, somehow, and out into the main harbour. But how could that be, if they'd been blown further up the Tiddle, to the west?

His mind reeled. It was no joke. If the boat went on the rocks at the mouth of the Tiddle, she'd smash herself to matchwood in no time. On the opposite side of the harbour was a steep breakwater, a sandy beach, and the entrance to the harbour. If you sailed out the entrance, Phonse liked to say, you'd cross the whole Atlantic Ocean before you saw land again. That was a scary idea.

But smashing the boat on the rocks was even scarier. Andrew knew that most boats are safe in open water, no matter how rough it is. Most boats will take more punishment than their crews. If the worst came to the worst, Andrew decided, they could just jill around all night and find their way back home in the morning.

What was that, off to port? It was gone again — no, there it was, an orange ball bouncing in the water. Denny had seen it, too.

"Jack Grant's buoy," grunted Denny.

"Maybe," said Andrew. "But Charlie Johnston got one just like it, on the other side of the government wharf."

"Better keep joggin'," said Denny. "Could tie up to it, but most of them buoys are only to hold dories. They wouldn't hold this big boat."

"And we got no anchor," said Andrew gloomily. "Dad took it up to get it welded and never got a chance to bring it back aboard."

"Keep her headin' east," said Denny. "No great danger down in that end of the harbour. How are we fixed for gas?"

"Plenty," said Andrew. "And an extra can back in the stern, too."

How much headway were they making, idling into the wind? The motion of the boat seemed different somehow. What if the wind was blowing hard enough to hold them in one spot? What if they were losing ground, being blown backwards? Andrew couldn't see a thing. He had no way to judge.

The boat *was* moving differently, rising and falling far more heavily, plunging into the waves. They must be right in line with the harbour mouth, so that the wind was sweeping straight in from the open ocean.

Andrew swung the spotlight around and froze stiff at what he saw. Just to starboard a huge plume of white water shot into the air where a big wave smashed on a sunken rock. But there were no rocks that size inside the harbour.

"Holy snappin'!" breathed Denny.

The wind screamed now, and the boat was smashing up and down like a huge rocking horse. The seas were heavy and angry, and the wind was tearing and plucking at the boat. Where were they, and how had the sea become so much more ferocious?

"There's a red light," said Denny, pointing. "It's gone. No, there it is again. Gone again. Now."

Andrew followed his cousin's finger. The red light was flashing to starboard. What was the rule? You were supposed to keep the red buoys on your right, but was that on the way out of the harbour, or on the way back in? Think, Andrew, he told himself. Then he heard Phonse's voice: *The three R's, Andrew. Red to right, returning.*

So the red buoy should be on his left, since he wasn't coming into Widow's Harbour. But it was on his right. He whirled the wheel and steered for the light. The boat was bucking and rolling, fighting the wheel. Andrew braced his feet apart. The boat was moving at an angle to the waves, making a terrible twisting motion, smashing the seas with her port bow, rearing up her starboard quarter as the waves rolled under her and away.

Denny rushed to the side of the boat, hung on for dear life, and was horribly sick over the side. Andrew looked at him sadly, wondering what he could do, and realized he couldn't do anything.

The buoy! They were right on top of it. Andrew eased the boat along side of it and read the words *FRIGATE ROCK* in bold white letters on the tossing round base of the big steel structure. They were close enough to hear the *Klang! Klang!* of its bell, ringing each time a wave heaved the buoy over sideways.

"Frigate Rock," said Denny, coughing and spitting. "You know — what that means, Andrew."

"Yeah," said Andrew shivering. "Means we're outside the harbour. Out in the ocean."

They tried the radio. It was full of static and interference from the storm. They tried to turn back, but as soon as they put *Dolly C*'s stern to the waves, whitecaps rolled right into the boat, threatening to sink it.

"Nothing we can do but keep joggin' into it," said Denny. "Safest thing to do, anyways."

"Mom's gonna be some worried."

"Nothin' we can do about it," said Denny. "She'll just have to worry."

"Gonna be a long night," said Andrew.

8

DOLLY C smashed into a sea, shuddered, and almost stopped. She drew herself together, rose on the next sea, and wallowed down its back. White spray lost itself in the mist and rain as Andrew fought the wheel to keep her heading straight into the angry, tossing heaps of water. Denny was below, sound asleep. They had kept watch together until Andrew noticed Denny slumping against the instrument panel. Andrew reached out and shook Denny's shoulder.

"Whuu—?" said Denny.

"You're asleep, you mutt."

"Guess I was."

"Maybe you should go lie down," Andrew said hesitantly. "One of us got to be awake, and I reckon I can't last forever."

"I'm okay."

"Sure, but what about when we both get sleepy? You better get some sleep now, and I can sleep later."

"All right," said Denny, and he blundered down into the little cabin, drew a couple of old blankets around him, and slept.

Dolly C crashed into another foaming wall of water, and Andrew wondered whether he'd be able to stay awake all night. Not if he had to steer so hard all the time. Well, Denny could steer later. Good old Denny. Comical and careful and steady. Never got too excited.

Lift, slide, crash! Lift, slide, crash! Would the night never end? Far ahead he caught sight of a faint white flash. It faded, then reappeared. Must be another buoy. Well, at least it would tell him where he was. He adjusted his course slightly to steer for it. On its new course, the boat began a slightly different motion. It lifted, then fell away heavily to port as it rose over the waves. Like a corkscrew, thought Andrew, but at least it's a bit of a change from all that pounding.

The moments went by, and the winking white light drew nearer. Plunging through the seas, *Dolly C* shook and rolled her way toward the buoy. Soon it was close enough that its powerful flashing light lit up the inside of the wheelhouse. Andrew edged toward the buoy. Now, over the shriek of the wind, he could hear its deep sonorous moan as the hollow pipe inside it filled with water. "Groaners," the fishermen called these buoys. The buoy heaved and sobbed at Andrew again.

"C-F," he read at the base of the tower. Charlie Foxtrot buoy. Something inside him gave a little flip. Charlie Foxtrot was the last buoy in the big-ship channel heading up to Port Esperance. After this, *Dolly C* faced the endless ocean, wild and empty.

The boat took a dive to starboard, and a breaking wave slapped her port bow, turning her sideways. He fought the wheel to bring her back on course. If one of those big breakers caught *Dolly C* broadside on, it could roll her over sideways, smash in her windows, and send cascades of water flooding into her. Not many waves would have to sweep her before the weight of the engine and the fishing gear would sink her.

Andrew stared into the mist and spray, willing himself to stay awake. He made his eyes focus through the circle of the clear-view. Hard to keep looking when there's nothing to — see — except —

He snapped awake as the boat lurched quickly to starboard, rolling heavily. A roaring comber of a wave reared up out of the darkness on his left, broke, and came smoking down like an avalanche towards the little fishing boat. Andrew cried out, and then the wave lifted *Dolly C* up and heaved her sideways, pressing her whole starboard side into the ocean. Water poured into the open cockpit, and the deck slipped out from under his feet. Icy water raced around his ankles and splashed down the steps into the little cabin. Andrew heard himself moaning, and the boat hung on her side for what seemed like hours.

Then she rolled quickly back, the water sloshing in the cockpit and wheelhouse. Andrew reached forward, struggling for his footing, and the steady drumming of the engine rose to a roar as he twirled the wheel to port. *Crash!* The water flew outwards from her bow, and she shuddered. *Crash!* Andrew reached for the throttle again and slowed the engine down.

Denny was beside him, holding tightly to the grab-rail.

"Holy liftin' Moses!" Denny breathed. "What happened there?"

"Must have fallen asleep," Andrew said, embarrassed.

"Wakes a feller up pretty quick," said Denny shaking his head. "Dumped me right out of the bunk into a pool of water."

"Sorry, Denny," said Andrew feeling foolish.

"Would have made a good picture," Denny laughed. "Want me to steer? You need some sleep."

"Maybe later," said Andrew. "But right now she's heavy to steer. Must have some water in her, and I don't know if that electric pump is workin' or not."

"What if it ain't?"

"We pump by hand," Andrew laughed. "Dad always says that's the best pump there is — a scared man with a bucket."

"Gimme the wheel."

"Okay." Andrew reached out for the grabrail and slid sideways. "The tricky thing is, the wind is holding her almost dead in the water, so she won't answer the wheel the way she should. You really got to throw it over."

Andrew stayed and watched anxiously while Denny got the knack of waiting until the peak of each wave, sensing which way the boat wanted to turn, and then steering her firmly back into the oncoming seas. A wall of water roared out of the darkness, picking up *Dolly C*'s bow and lifting it like a potato chip. She rose to the top of the wave and began to slew to port. Denny swung the wheel to starboard.

"You got it," said Andrew. "I'm going below to check that pump."

Down in the cabin Andrew lay on the floor, rolled up his sleeve, and groped around in the stinking, oily water, grasping for the electric bilge pump. His hand swept around in circles, searching, then fetched up against something solid and round. The pump. It was vibrating, but the water around it wasn't moving. He swept his fingers around its base and found a lump of something soft clogging its intake. He pulled it free and felt the water flowing through his fingers as the pump started clearing the bilge. He rolled over and sat up. In his hand was a soggy lump of rags, hair, string, fish scales, and paper. He stood up, climbed out into the wheelhouse and threw it overboard. Grabbing a rag, he wiped his hands.

"Got 'er?"

"Yeah. Old lump of waste blocking the inlet."

Denny looked at him. "You should get a nap, too."

"Yeah," Andrew nodded, feeling a yawn working its way up into his throat. He took a look around and saw nothing but the wastes of heaving ocean, the crumbling white tops of breakers. "Call me if you need me, right?"

Down in the cabin he was asleep almost before he lay down.

Denny steered on, lifting and sliding and crashing over the seas. It was kind of lonely, but Andrew hadn't slept at all. Hard to tell how much time had gone by when nothing seemed to change. He swung the wheel this way and that, automatically, and his mind ranged all over the place.

How were their fathers making out in jail? What would their mothers be doing?

When daylight came, where would it find them?

Who had cut *Dolly C*'s mooring lines?

Strange how sleepy a person got, even in the wild lifting and smashing of the storm. But it had a rhythm, too. It rocked you to sleep, noisy though it was. Lift. Slide. Smash. Lift. Slide. Smash —

Denny blinked his eyes. Soon he'd be drifting off to sleep himself. The trouble was, there was nothing to see but mist and ocean, waves and spray. He kept straining his eyes, peering into the darkness.

The rain came back with a gust of wind that shrieked around the boat and rattled the glass in the side windows. Denny hung on and steered. Again he could see nothing beyond the bow of the boat but streaks of rain and dancing water. Lift, slide, smash! It was like a noisy, endless dance —

Denny woke up sharply as the boat slipped sideways and a crest exploded against the starboard bow. He fought the boat back on its course and then saw that the rain had eased off again. How long had he been asleep? Or had he only been dozing on his feet while his hands did their work?

He yawned, lifted his head, and looked around. Then he screamed.

"Andrew!!"

The lights were far above him, white over white, red beside green, the lights of a huge ship towering over *Dolly C.* At sea, on a night like this, the last thing they would be looking for would be a little wooden fishing boat —

"Andrew!!"

Andrew scrambled into the wheelhouse, shaking his head as though he were throwing the sleep out of it, and snapping, "What? *What?*"

"Ship!" cried Denny. Deep beneath his feet he thought he could feel the rumble of the ship's engines as it bore down on *Dolly C.*

"Holy liftin'! Let me in there!" cried Andrew, seeing the lights. Almost before the words were out of his mouth he had thrust Denny off the seat. *"Hold on!"* he cried, and spun the wheel to starboard while his other hand found the throttle and opened it wide. *Dolly C*

rolled her rail underwater again, and the engine roared.

"We're gonna roll her over!" Denny screamed.

"Only chance we got!" Andrew yelled.

Clutching the grabrail, Denny stared at the ship and saw its lights winking out. It must be right on top of them, its huge bulk between them and the lights. Suddenly they could see the angry white curl of the ship's bow as it pushed through the water. The ship rose behind it, a heavy blacker mass in the already black night. It was coming on at an enormous rate, heaving slowly from side to side. *Dolly C*'s engine was howling as it struggled to push the staggering little boat clear, but beneath its vibrations Denny could feel, through his feet, the steady throbbing *thump-thump-thump* of the big ship's propeller.

"We're gonna make it!" shouted Denny.

"Maybe!" Andrew yelled grimly. *"But—no, no, NO!"*

The huge rounded steel bow of the ship bore down on them, the bow wave reared above them, and the boys both screamed as the bow wave crashed into the cockpit. The tip of the bow passed behind them, but with a heavy thump the ship's wide flaring side hit them almost at the stern. *Dolly C* swirled sideways, rolled away from the ship and then back again, and Denny, clinging desperately to the grabrail, was thrown one way and then the other as *Dolly C* bumped along the endless length of the ship. Denny heard crashes, the sound of splintering wood and shattering glass. The sound of the ship's great propeller grew louder and louder until it filled the air like a gigantic heartbeat. *Dolly C* gave a couple of violent lurches, and the thumping grew fainter. Denny heard a voice screaming, and realized it was his own.

The ship had passed. As if in a nightmare, Denny saw her single white sternlight marching away into the night, rising and wiping the sky behind *Dolly C*.

"Andrew!" he heard himself screaming. "*Andrew!!*"

The wind and the sea screamed back at him.

Denny felt his knees go weak with fear and horror. Andrew must have gone overboard, and Denny was alone in a wrecked boat. And then he felt something soft and yielding, lying in the cold water that sloshed around his feet.

"Andrew!" he bent down and felt his cousin's face. Was Andrew alive? Denny bent right down beside him and heard Andrew's breath coming in long, ragged gasps. He's alive, anyways, Denny thought. He's knocked out. I got to get him down below. He slipped down into the cabin, bracing himself carefully, and pulled the mattresses and blankets down onto the cabin floor. Reaching out the door, he got a hand under each of Andrew's shoulders and drew him into the cabin. He lost his balance and toppled over backwards into the mattresses with Andrew on top of him. It took a moment to work his way out of the tangle.

He went up to the wheelhouse and realized the

engine was still racing, out of gear. *Dolly C* lay broadside to the waves, taking care of herself. And we were so scared of getting her broadside, thought Denny. Without the motor she takes a little water, but she's all right. He throttled back the engine, groped for a flashlight in the box by the steering wheel, and went below again.

Andrew was sleeping peacefully now, his breath coming and going in long, regular sighs. His face was bruised and bloody, but he seemed all right. Where was the blood coming from? Denny looked again and saw no injury. Yet Andrew's face was covered with fresh blood. With a start, Denny realized it was coming from his own cut hand — a long angry cut oozing blood from his wrist to his knuckles. He looked around and found an old rag, wrapped that around his hand, and used his teeth to tie it tight.

Back in the wheelhouse, Denny surveyed the damage. The whole port side of the house was smashed askelter, its windows shattered, its framing cracked. When the boat rolled and the waves struck the port side, he could see water running down inside the wheelhouse where it had pulled away from the deck. Back aft, the side deck was splintered and cracked, but the basic line of the boat seemed all right.

He took the wheel, put the motor in gear, and turned the boat into the seas again. Everything seemed to work. The ship had almost missed *Dolly C*, but the boat had rolled back into the ship, and the glancing blows along the ship's side had damaged the upper part of the boat more than the hull.

I guess I just keep on, Denny thought. What else can I do, anyway?

Andrew was fighting in his dreams, fighting against a web of ropes that held him in the water while the tide was rising. A giant fist was slapping him this way and that, banging him sideways, and someone was mocking him cruelly. This is a dream, he thought, I know it's a dream, I can wake up. And then suddenly he was awake, in the slate grey light of an early morning under stormy skies.

"Denny?"

Denny's solemn face, streaked with dirt and blood, appeared in the hatchway.

"Andrew? You all right?"

"Sore," said Andrew. "Ow! My side hurts."

"We're near land," said Denny. "I can see it, but I can't see any way into the harbour."

Andrew pulled himself to his feet and crept up into the wheelhouse. The place was a horrible mess. Bits of cord and empty cans and bottles from the garbage box had spilled across the deck, mingling with splinters of broken glass and wood.

"Look over there," said Denny, pointing out the cracked windshield.

Half-dazed, Andrew looked at the smashed and buckled deck near the bow, then looked up and saw what Denny was pointing at. The rain had stopped, and the fog had lifted, though the wind was still howling. Along the shore, behind the great rocks and boulders and the huge waves kicked up by the storm, were brightly painted houses: red, green, purple, yellow, white. Not Widow's Harbour, but a place he had seen before, once. Last summer, maybe —

"L'Anse au Griffon!" he yelled. "I was in here with Dad!"

"Yahoo!" shouted Denny. "But how d'you get in there?"

Andrew looked again. The harbour mouth should be just over there, beyond the boulders being lashed by the waves. But all he could see was breaking seas.

"It's in there," he said. "But in a sea like this, it's breakin' right clean across the entrance."

"We can't go in there, can we? asked Denny. "Be like riding a surfboard in one of those TV shows about Hawaii."

Andrew thought for a moment. "We've got to try it. We can't have much gas left, and you can feel how heavy she is. She must have a pile of water in her."

"Anyplace else we can go?"

"Not along here. This is the only harbour anywhere around here."

"You better do it," said Denny. "You've been in here before. And it's your boat."

Andrew moved his back and shoulders, flexed his

legs. Everything seemed to work. He knew Denny was right.

"All right, I'll do it."

His heart jumped as he said it. Denny slid off the seat, and Andrew took the wheel. Phonse had shown him the landmarks. The water tower, he could see that one clearly. That was one of them. And the other was — the church steeple, that's right. Get them lined up, the tower behind the steeple, and you can follow them right into the harbour.

He motored slowly along the shore, watching the steeple gradually moving into line with the water tower. He was going to have to turn hard and go in with the waves, riding them through the narrow gap between the rocks.

People were gathering along the bald, rocky shore. They were waving at him and trying to make signals, but he couldn't figure out what they were trying to tell him. *Dolly C* wallowed slowly along, just outside the surf. Great green masses of water rolled under her and then curled over on themselves and raced straight into the harbour, foam sliding down their backs like the white manes of wild horses. Andrew remembered a TV show on running through rapids in a canoe. That was what it would be like.

He was trembling and shaking, but he felt cold and steady inside. He knew what he had to do, and he knew it would soon be over.

Inside the harbour he saw another fishing boat, much like *Dolly C*, leaving a wharf and trying to come out towards the entrance. The other boat circled once inside the harbour and then rushed at the breaking seas. But the first breaker caught her and made her rear right back up on her stern. She crashed down into the next wave, which picked her up and carried her sideways, skidding along with the wave. She was away over on her side, her red bottom paint turned up towards *Dolly C*.

"Lord liftin'," breathed Denny.

"She's goin' right over!" Andrew muttered.

But when the wave flattened out inside the harbour, the boat came right side up, riding low in the water. The boys could see the men in it working frantically, and a stream of water poured out of the boat's side as the men worked at the pumps and steered slowly back towards the wharf.

Dolly C was on the fourth wave out now, being carried slowly sideways even as the engine drove her ahead. Andrew swung the wheel fast, and the boat straightened out as it fell heavily into the trough. Andrew glanced over his shoulder. Towering over the stern, the next wave approached. His stomach clenched itself up like a fist. There could be no turning back now. It was time to make his move.

Andrew's fear loosened as the stern of *Dolly C* rose up the face of the mighty breaker. He gunned the engine, and the boat surged forward. Time seemed to slow down as he felt the whole boat shiver in the grip of the sea, trembling as though she were trying to decide which way to turn. With the water running faster than the boat, the rudder was almost useless, but as the boat began falling off to starboard, Andrew turned hard to port, and *Dolly C* held almost straight. The foaming white crest was rushing along right beside the wheelhouse now, higher than the side of the boat. It rushed on past the boat and left it behind.

Again the boat wallowed in the trough, and Andrew fought the wheel to keep her heading straight into the narrow gap of the harbour entrance. Another huge breaker reared up over the stern. It broke, and a smother of foam burst over the after deck, into the cockpit and up around his ankles. But *Dolly C* was hurrying forward again, surfing once more on the peak of the wave as the water ran back along the cockpit floor and out through the drains. This time the boat wanted to go to starboard, and Andrew had to twirl the wheel to port. Denny was muttering under his breath.

They were in the narrow mouth of the harbour now, and Andrew could see the horrified faces of the men and women standing on the rocks outside their houses. He was amazed at how slowly everything seemed to be happening, at just how much time he seemed to have to decide when and how to move the wheel. When the second wave passed, *Dolly C* settled behind it almost inside the calm water of the harbour, her engine straining.

"Come on, baby!" cried Denny.

The third wave came right aboard like a raging animal, poured over the whole stern of the boat, knocked it sideways, rolled *Dolly C* down on her side and flooded the wheelhouse. Andrew cried out, and the water poured down into the cabin as the boat heaved farther and farther until solid water burst through the side window and pinned Andrew against the steering wheel.

This is the end, Andrew thought, *this wave is going to roll us over and over and over like a bottle on the beach, and we nearly made it, too. But we did the best we could, and it's not our fault.*

And then *Dolly C* slowly righted herself, water pouring off her as though she were a submarine rising to the surface, and then she was on her feet again, right side up, rocking sluggishly in the gentle swell of the harbour. The engine was dead, and the boat was low and full of water. Andrew closed his eyes, took a deep shuddering breath, and began to sob in a mixture of fear and relief and exhaustion.

"Hey, Andrew," Denny sobbed. "Hey, Andrew! Hey, Andrew!" Andrew felt his cousin pounding him on the back, and everything seemed far away.

Then he felt a heavy thump and another, and two boats were alongside *Dolly C.* Big fishermen in oil-skins and boots were jumping over the side and into *Dolly C,* and two of them charged into the wheel-house.

"By de saints!" roared a big fisherman in a red

and black jacket. "By de saints, by de saints, by de saints!" And he picked up Andrew and hugged him.

Things happened fast after that. Narcisse Le Blanc the big man, got *Dolly C* towed over to a wharf, and his friend Pascal called to the people ashore to put an electric pump aboard to clear the water out of her. When Andrew and Denny climbed up onto the wharf, they found it jammed with people. "Lemme check over that motor," said one man, pushing past them. "I'm a mechanic from the pulp mill." The people on the wharf seemed to be from all over Nova Scotia, and they were carrying signs that said *SUPPORT THE FISHERMEN* and *CHEMICAL WORKERS ON SYMPATHY STRIKE* and *RECOGNIZE ALLIED FISHERMEN'S UNION*. Men with cameras were taking pictures. As the boys came up the ladder, the crowd gave a great cheer.

"What's that for?" asked Denny.

"For you!" cried Narcisse. "Everybody knew you had to be out there at sea! There was a lot of praying going on."

Narcisse and Pascal shouldered their way through the crowd to a building, and put the boys on the phone to their mothers. Laura was laughing and crying when she talked to Andrew, and she kept saying, "I can't believe it, I can't believe it. I was sure you were drowned." Then the boys were outside again, and Narcisse was pulling them to a staircase and up to a landing halfway up the building, looking down on the crowd. Andrew had never seen so many people in one place. They were jammed along the wharf, on the road, in the parking lot, standing in the backs of trucks.

"Why are all these people here?" Andrew asked.

"When your father went to jail," said Pascal, "union people shut down half the companies in Nova Scotia, and come down 'ere to walk on the picket lines wit' us. If that judge t'ought he'd stop picketing by jail sentences, he must be thinkin' now about how wrong a man can be!"

Narcisse was holding up his hand for silence, and the crowd grew quiet.

"You know about Phonse and Leo Gurney, that's in jail!" he shouted. "Them are two brave men! Well, you seen that little boat come in 'ere just now, that was Phonse and Leo's sons, and they're two brave men, too!"

The crowd shouted and clapped.

"Wit' men like that, and wit' all you people behind us, we can't lose!" Narcisse cried. "I want you to let the boys know how much we t'ink of them!"

A great wave of shouting and whistling and cheering burst from the crowd as Narcisse took Andrew's and Denny's hands and held them up as though they were prizefighters.

"You say somet'ing," whispered Narcisse to Andrew, as the cheering died down.

There was so much to say, Andrew thought. About the whole long fight for the union, about Father

149

Guthrie, about the jail sentences, about the cut mooring lines on *Dolly C*, and he couldn't think of how to say any of it.

"We want our union," he said finally, and then realized he'd better shout.

"We want our union!" he shouted. "And I want my dad back from jail! And if all you people want that, too, then they should give it to us!"

The crowd gave another great roar, and Andrew swayed on his feet. His body felt like it was quitting, it couldn't stand up any more. Pascal caught him, and Narcisse took his other arm. Someone else was walking beside Denny down the staircase.

"We're gonna get you home," said Narcisse, "and right now, too. But it's good that crowd got to see you, anyways. They're some proud of you two."

As he bundled them into a van, Andrew caught a glimpse of poor old *Dolly C*, with her splintered deck and cock-eyed wheelhouse. A gang of men were winching her up a slipway. Pascal saw where he was looking and laughed.

"Next time you see dat boat," he said, "you're gonna t'ink she's brand-new! What a job we'll do onto her!"

"She's a — good — boat," Andrew muttered. They laid him down on a bed in the back of the van, and laid Denny beside him. They were both asleep before the van pulled out of L'Anse au Griffon for the long drive up and down the bay to Widow's Harbour.

"Shock and exposure," said Dr. Springer, smiling

down at Andrew. "A day in bed, lots of sleep, hot soup. He'll be A-1 tomorrow. You're all made of rubber and leather, young man."

Andrew smiled. The doctor seemed very distant. He wriggled his toes in the sheets. His bed was unbelievably soft, lusciously warm.

It had been a crazy day. There'd been even more people in Widow's Harbour than in L'Anse au Griffon. The whole street in front of the plant had been full of people. Reporters with microphones had crowded around as the van stopped in front of the house to let the boys out.

"What was it like out there?"

"Were you frightened?"

"Why didn't you call for help on the radio?"

"Why did you decide to go to sea?"

Narcisse had brushed them aside. "You guys talk to dem later, eh? They're tired, and they ain't seen their mothers yet." Laura had hugged him, laughing and crying. Dr. Springer had come along right after that. Andrew felt himself slipping into sleep —

Later he woke up, had some soup, heard excited voices talking downstairs, and drifted back to sleep. At supper time, he went downstairs to watch the TV news. The living room was jammed with people, most of them strangers. The big story was the strike, and the sympathy strikes across the province, and the mobs of people on the picket lines in the two little fishing ports. The newscaster came on to say that the government was worried and would probably have to do something to get the province's labour force back to their jobs.

"The crisis resulted from the sentencing of Phonse Gurney, 43, of Widow's Harbour, to eight months' imprisonment," said the newscaster. "Meanwhile, in Widow's Harbour, Gurney's boat went adrift with his son and nephew aboard. Andrew Gurney, 13, and his cousin Dennis, 14, rode out last night's storm in the open sea off the Eastern Shore, and this morning made port with the boat damaged by a collision with a tanker at sea. They were given a hero's welcome in L'Anse au Griffon, where they landed."

As he said this, the screen showed the massive breakers at the harbour mouth, and then *Dolly C* came into view, riding on a crest. She looked like a toy boat, and her bow stood straight up in the air and then plunged down again. When the next wave broke, the stern of the boat disappeared and she slewed sideways, and the camera showed the top of the wheelhouse pointing sideways into the harbour.

Everyone in the room murmured, and Laura dug her fingers into Andrew's shoulder, holding him tight.

Then the TV showed Andrew and Denny with Narcisse and Pascal, and Andrew speaking to the crowd.

"We want our union!" shouted the boy on the TV. "And I want my dad back from jail! And if all you people want that, too, then they should give it to us!"

As the crowd roared, the picture faded, and the newsman came back on the screen.

"Andrew Gurney, in L'Anse au Griffon. In other news, three people died in a head-on collision —"

Someone stood up and snapped off the TV.

"I'm glad that was you comin' in there, not me," said John Cavanaugh. "How did that boat get loose, anyway?"

Andrew shrugged. Good question, he thought. We'll see about that.

Then everyone was at him with questions, and he was doing his best to talk to three or four people at once.

"Andrew!"

He looked up. Scott was at the door with his mother and father! He pushed people aside and forced his way to the door.

"Wow!" said Scott. "How'd you do it? You all right? Where's Denny? When —"

"Slow down!" Andrew laughed. "Look, we got to —"

"Father Guthrie!" called Denise. "What did the bishop say?"

Father Guthrie smiled, and the room went completely silent.

"The bishop wanted me to move," he said, "until I showed him the petition. That made him think again. After that we had quite a long talk, and in the end he said he thought we shouldn't make a hasty decision. I asked him what he meant, and he said he thought perhaps I should stay where I was for at least another six months, probably longer."

The room exploded with cheers and whistles. People clapped their hands and stamped their feet.

After things quietened down, a man's voice said, "And then you get out?"

"I don't think so," said Father Guthrie. "I think he'll just quietly forget about the idea of moving me."

There were more whistles and cheers. Andrew took Scott by the elbow and drew him into a corner.

"Listen," he said, "we can't talk here. But we got some work to do. First thing in the morning, you get hold of Denny and bring him over here. Bring your diving gear, will you?"

"Sure," said Scott. "What —"

Andrew shook his head. Someone else was tapping him on the shoulder.

"First thing in the morning. Don't forget."

9

ANDREW woke up full of energy. The sun was not far above the horizon, and the dewy grass was sparkling with golden light. He slipped downstairs. Someone was sleeping in the hall, and he could see bodies wrapped in blankets and sleeping bags on the living-room floor. In the kitchen, a tall, grey-haired man was pouring a cup of tea.

"Hello, young Andrew," he said. "You're up early."

"Things to do," said Andrew.

"Want a cup of tea?" asked the man. "By the way, I'm Henry Driscoll, from Dartmouth."

"Hi." Andrew took the cup of tea, got himself a bowl of cereal, and wolfed it down.

"What's the hurry?" asked Driscoll.

Andrew shrugged. Then he heard a light tapping on the back door. Scott came in with Denny behind him. Andrew stood up.

"If Mom's looking for me, tell her I'm with Denny and Scott," he said to Driscoll. "Come on, let's go."

Scott had his bag of diving gear just outside the door.

"What's up?" asked Denny.

"Come on down to the wharf," said Andrew leading the way. He said nothing more until he got down on the wharf where *Dolly C* belonged. He hardly noticed the tents and campers all around the place. Then he turned and faced Scott and Denny, his face set. In a few minutes he might have some answers.

"Remember that night we went aboard, Denny, you kicked somethin' off of the wharf?"

"Yeah, I remember."

"Shouldn't be anything loose on the wharf," said Andrew. "Dad's right fussy about that. Whatever it was that Denny kicked over, I want to see it."

"You think it might be a clue?" said Scott.

"Might be," said Andrew. "Who cut that boat adrift, anyways? I can't see nothin' else that could tell us."

All three boys moved over to the side of the wharf and looked down. They saw dark green water and nothing else. The bottom was completely hidden.

"Sometimes you might see somethin'," Andrew said. "But the water's right cloudy this late in the summer."

"I can change in the shed," said Scott excitedly.

Andrew unlocked it, and Scott went in.

"Really think we'll find anything?" asked Denny.

"Worth a try," said Andrew. "And the sooner the better."

Scott entered the water beside the wharf, gave a little gasp as it filtered into his wetsuit, and then flopped face down, breathing through his snorkel and kicking smoothly around to the face of the wharf. He stopped at a ladder, and lifted his face out of the water.

"Can't see much," he called. We need a rock or something to carry me down."

"I'll get a trawl anchor from the shed," Andrew said.

"Where did you kick that thing off?" Scott asked, as Andrew trotted across the wharf.

"Somewhere around where you are," Denny said. "Don't know any closer 'n' that."

Andrew came back with a small anchor and a length of rope.

"This do you?"

"I think so. Drop it over. Hey! Not on my head!"

"Sorry," Andrew steadied the anchor against the wharf and slid it down to Scott. Scott grabbed it, grinned, took three deep breaths, put his snorkel back in his mouth, and nodded. Andrew let go of the rope, and Scott vanished into the dark green water. Some bubbles broke the surface. Then Scott's head burst into the air, breathing deeply.

"Nothing," he gasped. "Try again." Andrew hauled

up the anchor, waited for Scott's nod, and dropped it. Scott went down again. After four dives he had found nothing.

"Maybe it was just a rock," said Denny. "Or a piece of wood or something."

"Maybe," coughed Scott, blowing water out of his mouth, "But we've only looked at a little piece of the bottom. What if we try farther out?"

"Can't be too far out," said Andrew. "The boat was close enough to jump aboard, and the thing fell in between that and the wharf."

"Wish we knew what we were lookin' for," said Denny.

"Just lookin' for anything out of the way," said Andrew.

"Let's try some more," said Scott. "Lemme see that anchor."

He took the anchor in his hand, and pushed himself off from the wharf, aiming for the bottom a little further out. When he came back up the next time, he nodded.

"Got out a lot further," he said. "Water's a good bit deeper out there."

"Want to go again?" Andrew asked.

Scott nodded. Andrew let some slack fall into the rope, and Scott plunged out from the wharf again. The other two watched his bubbles. He seemed to stay down a long time.

Scott came back through the surface like a rocket, sucking furiously for air, and thrashing about with

his left hand. Tipping onto his side, he swam for the ladder.

"Got it!" he cried. He held up his hand . In it was a huge knife.

"A *baitchopper?*" said Denny. "Yeah, that'd cut them mooring lines clean as a whistle!"

"Which is how they were cut!" Andrew said excitedly. "Remember? One slash is all it took. No sawing away at them. Well, look!" In two strides he was at the edge of the wharf. The cut lines were still hanging uselessly over the wharf. They were chopped right through.

Scott padded around to the side of the wharf and up to the shore. He lifted his mask and snorkel off his face and the three of them gathered around to look at the knife. It was as long as Scott's arm, with a heavy wooden handle and a long, wickedly sharp blade. Scott turned it over.

"Hey! There's markings on it!"

"A.H." read Scott.

"Ambrose Hendsbee!" said Andrew.

"Nobody else around with them initials," said Denny. "And I seen him usin' that baitchopper, too."

"Let's go," said Andrew grimly. Take it easy, he told himself. Temper is a luxury.

They could hear the sound of the whooping and cheering before they got anywhere near the house, and it was answered by happy shouts from the picket

160

line down on Water Street. People were flowing out of Andrew's house, and when Denise Ryan saw the three of them, she rushed over and hugged Andrew, lifting him right off his feet and swinging him around, laughing and shouting. Andrew was almost smothered.

"What's going on?" he heard Denny yelling.

"*We won, we won, we won!*" cried Denise. "*We won!*"

"What?"

"We did?"

"What happened?"

"The premier was just on TV, and he said they're putting in an emergency law to give bargaining rights to fishermen, and the men are getting out of jail this afternoon! Your Dad'll be home tonight!"

"*Wahoo!*"

"*Yeaaaaaaay!*"

"Slow down, Scott!" snapped Denise. "You're going to chop somebody's head off with that thing!"

"Sorry," said Scott blushing. Andrew looked at him and almost laughed. Scott was standing there dripping wet in his black diving suit, waving his mask and flippers in one hand and the baitchopper in the other.

"What on earth are you doing with that thing, anyway?" asked Denise.

"You seen Ambrose Hendsbee?" Andrew asked.

"Yeah, he's around here somewheres. Why?" asked Denise.

"I wanna talk to him."

"Isn't that him comin' around the house?" asked Denny.

"Yeah. With Ernie."

Andrew stormed over to Ambrose with the others following along behind. He reached out his hand, and Scott gave him the baitchopper. Andrew marched straight up to Ambrose and stopped him.

"This your baitchopper?" he asked.

"Yeah," said Ambrose. Ernie turned red and started to run.

"Grab him," said Scott, and Denny tackled Ernie and brought him down. Scott leaped on the two of them, and they held Ernie still.

"Leave that boy alone!" snapped Ambrose. "And gimme that baitchopper. I been wonderin' where it got to since a couple of days."

Andrew pulled the knife back from Ambrose's outstretched hand.

"Listen," he said, "this is the knife that cut *Dolly C*'s lines the other night. So I guess we know who cut her loose."

"I don't know nothin' about it!" Ambrose cried. "I told you, that knife's been missin'!"

"Then why did Ernie want to run?" Denise asked.

"You said it!" Ernie shouted at Ambrose. "You said it!"

"What did I say?" snapped Ambrose.

"After Phonse got jailed, you said, *Now if a few of them inshore boats got smashed up they'd give up this foolish strike,*" said Ernie. He was crying. "You said, *That'd be the best thing could happen right now.*"

"So you went and started cuttin' 'em loose, did you, you little rat?" cried Denise. She started for him and Ernie wriggled furiously. He took Scott and Denny by surprise and threw them off. Half crawling, half running, he got out of their reach and raced away down the street into the crowd of people. Denise was still screaming at him.

Ambrose suddenly ran at Andrew, grabbing for the big knife. He caught Andrew's T-shirt, but Andrew pulled away and heard the shirt rip right off his back. With Ambrose running hard behind him, Andrew raced for the wharf and hurled the bait-chopper far out into the harbour.

"What'd you do that for?" puffed Ambrose. "Now you got no evidence."

"Scott can get it again," smiled Andrew. "But you can't. Anyway, who needs evidence? You showed us what a skunk you are. We don't need to prove it."

With a roar of rage Ambrose ran at Andrew again. Andrew sidestepped, and Ambrose skidded to a halt right at the edge of the wharf. Denny was running down the wharf to help. He couldn't stop. He ran straight into Ambrose.

Very, very slowly, Ambrose fell over sideways, clawing the air and fighting to keep his balance. He teetered over the edge, his arms going like a windmill, and then he lost his balance completely and fell over the side of the wharf. The splash showered the people on the wharf with drops of water.

Andrew looked around. The wharf was crowded with people, and they were all shaking with laughter as Ambrose thrashed the water and made his way to shore. Dripping wet, he slunk away with the laughter ringing in his ears.

Nobody laughed harder than Phonse and Buck when they made it home late that night. Everyone went down to the rectory and gathered around the piano. Buck got out his guitar, and one of the paper-mill workers had a fiddle, and everyone ate and drank and danced and sang until the short summer night was gone. When Andrew and his parents went out on the rectory porch to go home, the darkness had vanished, and the sky was streaked and banded with gold and rose.

"Aaaah!" sighed Phonse, stretching. Andrew looked out over the placid harbour with its tethered boats, and on out to the island with its green ruff of spruce trees.

"Beautiful morning," said Phonse. "Look, here comes the sun."

Far out to sea, a burning point of light appeared on the eastern horizon. It became an arc and then a semi-circle. Then, suddenly, the whole round golden ball seemed to jump right up and out of the ocean, bathing the world in the warm, soft light of a new and glowing day.

Glossary

Baitchopper. A sharp knife used to cut up fishing bait.

Bilge. The flat, bottom part of a boat.

Bow. The front end of a boat or ship.

Breaker. A heavy ocean wave that breaks on the coast or over reefs. A comber.

Breakwater. A wall or barrier that is built to stop the force of incoming waves.

Brine. Very salty water.

Buoy. A floating object, anchored to the bottom of the sea, which marks an object or location of importance to mariners.

Clearview. A circle of glass in a boat's windshield which is spun rapidly by an electric motor in order to keep that part of the windshield clear of rain, spray, snow, etc. It performs the same job as a windshield wiper, but it removes amounts of water that would overpower a wiper.

Cockpit. The open area, generally in the stern of a boat, in which the boat's work is done. In a fishing boat, nets are hauled and fish cleaned in the cockpit.

Comber. A long, curling wave that rolls over or breaks at the top. A breaker.

Delegation. A group of people who represent or express the opinions of a larger group of people.

Dory. A specialized rowboat with a narrow flat bottom and high flaring sides.

Dragger. A fishing boat that drags large nets over the bottom of the ocean. A trawler.

Ex parte motion. An action in court made in the interests of one side only.

Gale. A very strong wind.

Gillnets. Nets that trap fish by catching on their gills as the fish try to pass through the net.

Injunction. A court order that commands people to stop doing something.

Jetty. A landing dock that juts out into the water.

Jigger. A fishing tackle that consists of a hook or bait on the end of a small cast lead weight. It is used by lowering overboard and "jigging" up and down to attract fish.

Jigger mast. The small mast in the stern of a powerboat, used chiefly to steady the boat's motion, or to make the boat steer herself.

Legislature. The group of people who make the laws in a province.

Mooring lines. The ropes used to anchor a boat or ship, or to hold it to a wharf.

Outboard. A boat with an outboard motor, a self-contained unit clamped to the stern.

Petition. A written request for something, usually signed by a group of people.

Pollack. A saltwater fish similar to cod.

Port. The left side of a boat or ship, when one is facing the front.

Rectory. A house owned by a church, where the minister or priest of the church lives.

Remand. To send someone back into prison, without sentencing, until further investigation has been made into a case.

Samson post. A large, strong post that passes through the deck, usually the forward deck, of a boat or ship. It is used to fasten mooring lines.

Scab. A person who refuses to join a strike or who takes the place of a worker who is on strike.

Slipway. A ramp on the shore up which a boat may be drawn on to the land for storage or repairs.

Snorkel. A curved rubber tube that lets swimmers breathe underwater while they are swimming near the surface.

Starboard. The right side of a boat or ship, when one is facing the front.

Stern. The rear part of a boat or ship.

Summons. An official order to appear in court.

Trawler. A fishing boat that catches fish by dragging large nets along the bottom of the sea. A dragger.

Trawl line. A long fishing line held up by a buoy. The main line has short lines running from it, and there are baited hooks at the end of these lines, which catch the fish.

Tee-totally. Completely. Absolutely.

Throttle. The valve that controls the flow of gas in an engine and thereby controls the engine's speed. A gas pedal in a car is a form of throttle.

Wetsuit. A skin-tight rubber suit worn by divers.

Wheelhouse. A small sheltered cabin where the steering wheel of a boat is located.

Winch. A machine for lifting or pulling objects.